Death With Blue Ribbon

Carolus Deene becomes involved in his latest adventure when a famous restaurateur is threatened by a protection racketeer. Then a well-known gourmand is murdered under extraordinary circumstances. Carolus's investigations in the world of pretentious catering lead him into great personal danger—horrifically so when a second murder, that of a member of the protection-racket gang, takes place.

Discovering the connection between two such seemingly disparate crimes, and extricating himself from tricky situations, Carolus exploits his *penchant* for solving mysteries in masterly fashion—aided and abetted by an author with a sure satirical touch and a nice sense of humour.

T0149818

Death With
Blue Ribbon

Leo Bruce

Academy
Chicago
Publishers

Published in 1994 by
Academy Chicago Publishers
262 West Erie Street
Chicago, Illinois 60610

Library of Congress Cataloging-in Publication Data

Bruce, Leo, 1903-1980.
     Death with blue ribbon / Leo Bruce.
        p.   cm.
      ISBN 0-89733-345-4
      I. Title.
  PR6005.RG673D46 1990
   823'.912—dc20   90-228
                                     CIP

Death With
Blue Ribbon

One

A tall thin man in a well-cut morning suit sat at an ornate desk in his office facing two unexpected callers. He was trying to control the nervous tremors which were making his leg twitch.

'This is nothing short of blackmail!' he said in a voice which he hoped would sound firm.

One of his callers, a coarse-featured man in his middle thirties, laughed heartily. He slapped his knee and released his laughter with no inhibition. But his eyes did not laugh, the tall man noted. His eyes remained cold.

'Blackmail, eh? That's good, Mr Rowlands.'

'The name is Rolland,' said the tall man, making it sound very French.

'*Now*, it is. Yves Rolland. You were Ivor Rowlands not so long ago. But never mind about that. Let's get back to what we were discussing. Here are you, the owner of a very successful business. Everyone knows the Haute Cuisine Restaurant at Farringforth. Here are we, friendly callers who want to be helpful. And you talk about blackmail. I don't call that polite.'

He laughed again, less uproariously but with the same chilly fixed expression of the eyes.

'What you propose is that I should pay you protection money. Protection against what? *You're* the only people I need protection against!'

'Oh dear!' laughed the other who had given his name as Jimmie Rivers. 'But you've got something there, Mr Rowlands. You've stated the case in a nutshell. We supply the need for protection, as you call it, as well as a twenty-four-hour-a-day security service. That's a politer name. You need that service, Mr Rowlands, and you're going to need it a lot more.'

'It's monstrous. I shall report it to the police.'

'You really mustn't make me laugh like this. It's not good for me. The police! And what do you think they would do for you? Make a note of the matter. Ask you to report anything further. And meanwhile what should *we* be doing? It wouldn't look well at all for you to appear a changed man after you'd come out of hospital would it? Teeth all smashed, no nose to speak of, eyesight gone very likely—that's if there was anything to take to hospital, which I doubt. So what would you tell the police then? No, Mr Rowlands, let's talk sense. We're not begging. There are a lot of us. A lot of hungry mouths to feed. We're really giving you a chance . . .'

'You're threatening to beat me up if I don't buy you off?'

'Oh dear, no. I was only just saying what might happen if you mentioned to anyone, *any*one, even your wife, mind you, that we'd happened to be passing and called in for a chat. I haven't introduced my friend, by the way. This is "Razor" Gray. Mr Rowlands. Razor's not very talkative—except when he's called upon.'

The third man made no acknowledgement of the introduction but continued to regard Rolland with contemptuous hostility. He was seedy in appearance but looked as though he had strength of the steel wire kind.

'Oh no,' went on Jimmie Rivers cheerfully. 'Nothing violent about us except in cases of emergency, like when silly chatter

8

has to be stopped. We're business men. We offer a complete security service. Security for *you* against any mishaps which might leave you disfigured, crippled, blind or otherwise incapacitated, and security for your business against any little trouble in your restaurant, causing inconvenience to your customers, like food poisoning and so on.'

'Food poisoning?' gasped Rolland.

'Just an illustration. Suppose someone ate something which caused sudden vomiting and made a claim for damages and that. See what I mean? Never do with a restaurant called the Haute Cuisine, would it? Or one or two coming in, like me and Razor might, and causing trouble, breakages, people hurt, when all your customers had expected was to dine quietly in a nice place like this. You know how these things might blow up if there happened to be a party of four, say, looking for trouble. You'd be covered against all that.'

'But no one makes trouble here.'

'That's not to say they wouldn't, is it? We wouldn't want you to have that sort of headache, Mr Rowlands. Ours is a very comprehensive service. Just like an insurance policy, really.'

Rolland seemed to be collecting himself for a last stand.

'And you provide the risks as well,' he said bitterly.

'Not if you were to use our service. But I haven't come to argue about it. I'm not a salesman. I'm doing you a good turn. Giving you a chance. All you have to do . . .'

'Yes?'

'Is pay. Our little charges are so moderate, really, when you think of the money you're making. You can't take it with you, you know.'

9

Pale and hoarse, Rolland asked, 'And what are those little charges?'

'Nothing really. Fifty a week. It's chicken-feed. Only you don't want to have to pay collection charges as well, do you? So we arrange to collect it as a lump sum in advance. One grand will keep you covered for twenty weeks. Nearly five months. Think of that. You wouldn't see us again till—where are we now? January the second—not till somewhere in May. Like the swallows. Back in the Spring.'

'I won't pay it. This can't happen in England.'

Jimmie Rivers started to laugh again. To say his laugh got on Rolland's nerves was a gross understatement. Rolland's nerves were stretched about as far as they would go.

'There you go again!' Rivers said. 'Wishful thinking. They *are* happening, Mr Rowlands. They happen every day in restaurants like yours. Classy, you know. Menu in French. Head waiter tarted up in tails. First-class *chef*. It's just where they *do* happen.'

'But why restaurants?' cried Rolland desperately.

'Oh, not only restaurants. Gambling clubs. Hotels. Casinos. Don't you read the papers? You're one of the lucky ones. Given a chance to use our service before anything happens. We haven't even given you a frightener yet.'

'A frightener?'

'You know. A little something to show which way the wind's blowing. Headlines like *Shots in Famous Restaurant*. The press get these things so quickly. I think you have a wonderful opportunity. What's fifty nicker? You spend that on electricity. But there you are. I shan't try to persuade you.'

'I haven't got a thousand pounds.'

'Of course you haven't!' said Rivers genially. 'Not in the till.

But there's plenty of time before the banks close. We could slip down together, couldn't we? I happen to know you have an account locally. No trouble at all. Only we should have to go at once. No point in wasting time. Razor and I have come a long way to do you this favour. We shouldn't want any messing about. Like telephoning anyone. Or chatting up the cashier at the bank. Just a quiet little transfer. Like you were drawing for wages, or New Year bonuses. All over in a minute until next May. You'd be able to sleep at night as sound as a baby. And may your restaurant continue to flourish!' he ended rhetorically.

Rolland, famous for his dictatorial behaviour with customers, the *restaurateur* who had earned headlines by telling a party to leave because one of them had asked for tomato ketchup with his *canard pressé,* a martinet with his highly-paid staff, now sat pale and sweating at his expensive desk. When he thought of the long climb into this position of wealth and authority it seemed even more fantastic that it should be threatened now by this confident and amused rogue and his sinister friend. Fantastic, yes, but it was not fantasy. All he had learned in his unscrupulous and utterly selfish career told him that he faced reality.

He looked back to his home in Woolwich and to his father, a professional waiter all his long working life, and to his own schooldays. He had not been a popular boy, having nothing, in schoolboy eyes, to justify his air of superiority. So far from feeling any indignation on his father's behalf for those years of meanly rewarded servitude, he had borrowed his life savings to start his first café and when this failed had made no attempt to repay the loan and watched his father spend the rest of his life keeping up a miserable show of respectability in conditions of semi-starvation. A series of dubious enterprises on borrowed money, tawdry little clubs full of *décor* and decadents, had brought him at last to acquaintance with Tony Brown in whom he recognised ability, for Tony was a born cook with a flair for artful catering. The two had decided on partnership on a fifty-fifty basis, Tony to run the kitchen of a restaurant they were to start and Rolland the business as a whole. They had planned to start in a small way and go forward cautiously.

They had actually found premises and paid a couple of thousand, supplied by Tony, for the lease when Rolland announced that he was about to marry a woman twenty years older than himself with a very large and unprotected fortune. He had bought the Fleur-de-Lys, an obscure pub thirty miles from London in a rift of unspoilt country and built onto it the splendid restaurant which he called the Haute Cuisine so that Tony, now known as Antoine, had no remedy but to become his *chef* at a high salary with a minute percentage of profits and no say in the business of which he was to have been part proprietor.

It was a squalid life-story but Rolland saw in it only his heroic career from modest beginnings to immense success. It was his shrewdness, his determination, his enterprise which had made him at less than forty years of age a famous *restaurateur* whose photograph and idealised biography had appeared in the illustrated supplement of a Sunday newspaper.

Though he had some knowledge of catering and menu language he would have puzzled a Frenchman, brought up in the tradition of real cooking, by his basic ignorance of the kitchen. But he made up for this in gastronomic arrogance and lectured his customers on wines and food, on what to drink with what, and on why his food was so much better than his rivals'. He had realised the value of a few specialities and had cashed in on one of those anomalies of taste and fashion by which *scampi* on a menu had become a status symbol in the English catering trade. He had been one of the first to import these mediocre shellfish frozen and had persuaded Antoine to produce a dish of them, deadened under a curried sauce with an admixture of coconut, *flambé* at the customer's table and called *Scampi à la Rolland*. It had helped to make his restaurant thrive.

Now, suddenly, today, soon after he had reached his office there had arrived out of the blue these two unwelcome callers. He had received them as he received all visitors on business, believing that they might offer him some opportunity for publicity. They had quickly disappointed his hopes and the man who called himself Jimmie Rivers had put forward his monstrous proposition as though it were a happy joke to be shared between them. But Rolland knew very surely that it was not a joke.

He tried to play it cool. He tried by his manner to show that he was not intimidated.

'And how would I know,' he asked coldly, 'that I was getting the benefits of this remarkable service you offer me?'

'You wouldn't,' said Rivers. 'You'd only know if you *weren't* getting it. You'd soon know that.'

'How soon?' he forced himself to ask.

'Could be tomorrow. Could be next day. But don't worry. There wouldn't be any doubt of it in your mind. That's one thing about us. We never leave any doubt in anyone's mind. Do we, Raze?'

The gentleman known as Razor Gray slowly shook his head. Once again Rolland tried to convince himself. This was

England. This could not happen here. Bank robberies, wage snatches, all that clumsy stuff, but a *protection* racket, as he had heard it called, that was only carried on in Chicago.

'Suppose I had not seen you this morning?'

He might have known this would make the fellow produce that ghastly laugh.

'Then you wouldn't have been warned, would you? We should have had to start straight away with the frightener, wouldn't we? What a lucky man you are!'

'I'm not going to do it!' said Rolland suddenly and loudly. 'You won't get a penny of mine. I'll have this place watched by the police. I'll employ tougher characters than ever you knew. You can get out, the pair of you.'

Strangely enough they both rose obediently as though they had been waiting impatiently for this, as though they hoped he would show defiance. They seemed quite willing to get their coats on and be gone.

Rolland, half relieved, half apprehensive, watched them. It was the apprehensive half that made him speak again, as though he wanted to delay them.

'You hear? Not a penny!' he said.

Rivers did not laugh again. He gave Rolland a pitying smile and went towards the door.

'Bye-bye,' he said amicably. 'Be seeing you.'

The two went out and it occurred to Rolland that he had not even noticed what car they drove and with what index number.

Suddenly he went into action. Someone else should share this—the horror, the humiliation, the anxiety, the fear. He went out to the kitchen. He saw that Antoine had just arrived.

'They're trying to blackmail me,' he said. 'Two of them. They want protection money.'

Antoine, a surly cadaverous fellow, showed no indignation or sympathy.

'How much do they want?' he asked.

'How much? What does it matter? You don't think I'm going to give in to *that*? It's scandalous. They talked of food poisoning.'

Antoine shrugged.

'This is England, not Chicago,' said Rolland. 'They can't do this to me. I shall employ a bodyguard. You must double all precautions. Inspect every piece of food that comes in. I'm going to the police.'

'You know your own business best,' said Antoine. It was evident that he meant to share none of the burden. 'I don't see what the police can do. What evidence is there?'

'Evidence? They told me straight out. A thousand pounds they wanted every five months.'

'I should pay it, if I were you,' said Antoine gloomily. 'You can afford it.'

'If *that's* your attitude . . .' began Rolland, but his one-time partner began to inspect some vegetables.

Two nights later a florid gentleman whom Rolland had never seen before was dining alone in the restaurant and ordered the *Scampi à la Rolland*. He had eaten about half of the portion allowed him when he suddenly changed colour to a dirty-brick red, his eyes bulged and he rose from his place and made for the gentlemen's lavatory where he could be heard vomiting violently.

There was an ugly scene in the foyer.

'I've been poisoned,' he said. 'That filthy fish. You'll hear more of this, I can promise you. How dare you give your customers food poisoning?'

A dozen expectant diners, waiting for tables in the crowded restaurant, looked startled.

'I assure you . . .' began Rolland.

'And I assure *you*,' interrupted the man, 'that you'll hear from my solicitors.'

He made for the door without leaving his card and walked away towards the car park.

There was only one thing for it. Rolland dare not—as he had admitted to himself in calmer moments—go to the police. A changed man after he came out of hospital, Rivers had said. What might happen if he mentioned it to anyone, *any*one? The police could not protect him. There was only one thing for it. A private detective. The name gave him a little relief. If he had Sherlock Holmes here, for instance, omnipotent, imperturbable Holmes. He was a character in fiction of nearly a century ago, but there must be someone to whom he could tell his appalling story.

Two

'So I'm prepared to spend a large sum, a really generous sum, to be rid of the whole thing,' said Rolland, expansively.

Carolus Deene examined his visitor without favour.

'It's what you might call a plum, this job,' went on Rolland. 'Free board at the Fleur-de-Lys. Free meals in the Haute Cuisine Restaurant—with the exception of certain starred dishes, of course. And a reasonable allowance of free drinks in the bar. *With* a large fee. Any private detective would jump at it.'

'But I'm not a private detective.'

'Not?' said Rolland. 'I understood that you were just the man for this job. I made enquiries before coming to see you. It needs someone presentable, as you can imagine. The Haute Cuisine has a reputation.'

'So have you,' said Carolus quietly. 'And it stinks.'

Rolland was never more surprised in his life. The words were spoken so indifferently and gently that he only just caught them.

He rose to his feet. He had endured a good deal in the last few days but this was too much. Some wretched little investigator insulting him like this.

'How dare you?' he asked.

'Sit down, you conceited fool,' said Carolus, but not altogether unkindly. 'Don't you realise I'm the only chance you've got? You're going to answer questions for the next ten minutes and I'll tell you whether I'll take the case or not. First I had better make something clear. The investigation of crime is a hobby with me but I have never looked at anything less than murder. I am rather inquisitive about that, I must admit. I'm a schoolmaster, you know, and I think it's answering the questions of small boys all term-time that makes me want to ask some of my own in the holidays. You haven't got a murder to offer me?'

'It's worse than murder. It's blackmail,' said Rolland.

'Still, one often leads to another,' Carolus reflected. 'You had better tell me all about it.'

He offered Rolland a cheroot and when he nervously refused, lit one himself.

Carolus was a spare muscular ex-Commando in his forties. His lovely young wife had died during the last war and he had remained a widower. The inheritance of what he described as an embarrassingly large income from his father had left him independent, but, unable to live in idleness, he had become senior history master at the Queen's School, Newminster, and fulfilled his duties conscientiously, though his colleagues viewed his Bentley Continental, his comfortable Georgian house, his reputedly self-indulgent way of living, cared for by his magnificent housekeeper Mrs Stick and her retiring but industrious husband, as unsuitable for one in his position on the staff.

The investigation of murder was his one interest outside the school. He applied a mind both scholarly and worldly to this and had been surprisingly successful in finding solutions to many puzzles connected with it. He had a quiet reputation as an investigator but never asserted himself. Two people claimed to disapprove of his criminological activities; his headmaster, Hugh Gorringer, who 'feared for the good name of the school they both served' as he put it, and Mrs Stick herself who did not like him to 'get mixed up in these nasty murder cases.'

Mrs Stick's facial expression when she had shown Rolland in that afternoon warned Carolus that she guessed the nature of his visit. She was a little woman, peering fiercely through steel-rimmed glasses, and her shrewish devotion to Carolus was not to be doubted.

Carolus had never listened more unwillingly to a recital of misfortunes, for Rolland showed the quality he most disliked— pretentiousness. But he had long believed that the protection racket was more common and more successful in England than was generally supposed and he was tempted to challenge it. He had no faith in the comfortable conviction of many people who read about it in newspapers that 'they only do it to their own kind.' He knew it to be a cruel and cunning form of crime, difficult to detect and sometimes impossible to bring to justice. So he encouraged Rolland to tell his story.

When he began with the visit of Rivers and Razor Gray a few days ago, Carolus drew him back to the past and in a few minutes had discovered, to his own satisfaction at least, how the Fleur-de-Lys Hotel had been purchased and the Haute Cuisine Restaurant added to it.

'What kind of pub was it before?' he asked.

'Oh, just a pub,' said Rolland. 'Nothing but local trade.'

He could not have said anything more calculated to lose the sympathy of Carolus.

'Nothing but local trade. I see. And what has happened to the "local trade" now?'

'We still get a few in the Georgian Lounge. The better type.

But we had to abolish the Public Bar. There simply wasn't room. They mostly go to the Black Horse at Netterly. It's three or four miles away, but they all have cars nowadays.'

'Go on, Mr Rolland.'

'Then I built on the restaurant. Georgian style. Chairs imitation Chippendale. Murals by a very clever lady artist representing hunting scenes. Silver . . .'

'I see it all,' said Carolus. 'You were successful from the first?'

'It took a lot of building up. But I'm pleased to say we are now one of the few Five Star restaurants in Great Britain, recommended by . . .'

'Yes. Yes. You have a good *chef*?'

'Antoine. I have to make suggestions, you know. But he can carry them out. And I have a first-rate head waiter. Stefan. He was at the Bordelaise for years.'

Rolland had mentioned one of the best restaurants in London.

'Why isn't he still there?'

'There was some trouble, I believe.'

'What trouble?'

'Stefan is temperamental.'

'You mean he drinks?'

'*I've* never seen any evidence of it. Well, nothing serious. Stefan . . .'

'Russian?' asked Carolus.

'No. Birmingham. His name's Stephen Digby. But he has *style*. I saw it at once and gave him a chance.'

'Very shrewd of you. You don't think he'll . . . let you down?'

'No. I've got him where I want him.'

'You're very frank. Who else is employed?'

'Two Moroccan waiters. Ali and Abdul. Stefan brought them back from Tangier. They don't have much to do with anyone. The customers seem to like them though. There's a wine waiter called Molt.'

'And in the kitchen?'

'Antoine's assistant Tom Bridger. Very good chap. Reliable. And an apprentice, David Paton.'

'All male?'

'No. There's a local woman for cleaning—Mrs Boot. And the barmaid, of course.'

'What about her?'

Rolland looked uncomfortable.

'Oh, she's just a barmaid. Manageress of the bar we call her.'

'What is her name?'

'Her professional name is Gloria Gee.'

'Very nice too. It goes with Stefan and Antoine. Is she young?'

'Under thirty.'

'Pretty?'

'I suppose so.'

'Get on with the customers?'

'As far as I know.'

'You seem to have a very satisfactory staff.'

'They want watching, of course. I have to be everywhere at once. If I didn't see to everything I might as well close down.'

'Now let's come to this visit you received.'

Rolland described it in detail, repeating with painful accuracy the words of Jimmie Rivers, which seemed to have burned themselves into his mind, as the saying goes.

'It must have been very uncomfortable.'

'It was a shock. But of course I absolutely refused to have anything to do with it.'

'And the two men went, without another word?'

' "Be seeing you", Rivers said.'

'But you haven't seen him since?'

'No. But two nights later this character appeared in the dining-room.'

Rolland described what had happened on that occasion.

'You thought he was just an ordinary customer?'

'Of course. Till the thing happened.'

'You are sure he wasn't—an ordinary customer?'

'I've told you, he made a scene.'

'Mightn't anyone if he thought he had been given food poisoning?'

'You don't mean you think the whole thing was unconnected with Rivers and his . . . threats?'

'I didn't say that. But there doesn't seem much evidence that the man himself was connected with them. I should be bloody angry if I was given something poisonous when I was paying your prices. How much *do* you charge for Dublin Bay prawns, or *scampi* as you call them?'

'Twenty-five bob. Stefan serves them from a chafing-dish.'

'Where do they come from?'

'Dublin Bay,' said Rolland.

'Then why call them *scampi*? They're frozen, of course?'

'Kept in the deep-freeze.'

'I see. And a customer got a wrong 'un. It could be that he did, you know. It would only take one to do it.'

'Impossible!' said Rolland.

'Not quite impossible. I'm not jumping to any conclusions,

Mr Rolland, but it is possible that one of those wretched prawns was deliberately "placed".'

'Oh God! You mean that one of the staff may have done it?'

'I only said it was possible.'

'But why? You don't mean that one of my employees may be working with Rivers?'

'How can we be sure? From what you tell me you're up against something pretty formidable.'

'Does that mean that you want to keep out of it?'

'Not necessarily. Look here, Rolland, I can't pretend I've got much sympathy for you. I don't like pretentious restaurants and phony French food. If I investigate this thing it won't be to save your bacon. But I happen to detest blackmail and I believe there is a whole organisation here dedicated to it. I shouldn't be surprised if half the smart restaurants in London were paying out to these people. That will never do, you know. It will mean more expensive food, for one thing. I'd like to know a great deal more about it.'

'You will come then? Can you come at once?'

'Why?'

'Because, by a most unfortunate coincidence (or perhaps the bastards knew), Imogen Marvell is coming down on Thursday.'

'Who is Imogen Marvell?'

Rolland goggled.

'You *don't know* who Imogen Marvell is? It's impossible! She's the greatest power in the world of gastronomy today.'

'Why?'

'She's the proprietor of *The Gourmet's Vade Mecum to the British Isles,* by far the most powerful of the guides. She leaves

Ronay and Postgate and the rest of them *standing*. She's the author of three coffee-table cookery books which have outsold Elizabeth David and Larousse. She opened the *Ma Façon* Restaurant in Chelsea three years ago and already there's a *Ma Façon* in Shepherd Market, Hampstead, Cheltenham, Bath and Tunbridge Wells, and she's opening them in Torremolinos and Ibiza. She's never *out* of the newspapers.'

'And what does she know about food?'

'Nothing,' snapped Rolland. 'But she writes about it, and broadcasts, and is photographed with it in colour. I hear she's making a full-length film of her gastronomic life. Last month she did her first programme on television and eight million people watched her cook Lobster Thermidor *à ma façon*. She's a tycoon.'

'What is she coming to your place for?'

'It's her annual visit for the *Gourmet's Vade Mecum*. She has to be treated like Royalty. If anything goes wrong while she is there it will be the end of the Haute Cuisine.'

'And you think I can prevent it?'

'You have said it. You're my one chance.'

'I can't prevent it, Rolland. I won't even undertake to try. If these men have got something planned for that day there is nothing I can do about it. What I will do is to come and stay at your pub and find out what I can. I won't accept your offer of free accommodation. I will take no responsibility at all. But I will come as an ordinary guest and perhaps, I can only say perhaps, I may help to break this thing up.'

'That's something,' said Rolland.

'It may take time. I can't promise you anything at all before Thursday when your visitor arrives. But I will come tomorrow.

All I ask is your authority to put any questions I like to anyone in the place.'

'Certainly. Certainly.'

'But I must warn you again that blackmail often leads to murder.'

Carolus had not noticed the entrance of Mrs Stick who had evidently caught the last words. She stared at Rolland with grim hostility as she set down the tray of drinks she carried.

'Will there be anything more, sir?' she asked Carolus as though she was a warder asking the last wishes of a man in the condemned cell.

'Thank you, Mrs Stick.' He looked at Rolland as though to enquire what his movements might be. 'A drink?' he asked.

'No thanks. I shall have to be getting back in a minute,' said Rolland.

'You must have a drink first.' He turned to Mrs Stick. 'I shall be out to dinner,' he said.

It was a subterfuge to prevent Rolland from staying on too long but Mrs Stick was disappointed.

'You didn't tell me, sir, and I was going to give you some nice foy dag no panny,' she said reproachfully, 'with free tots den dives.'

'Sounds delicious. We must have that another time. By the way, I'm going away tomorrow, Mrs Stick. I shall be staying at Mr Rolland's hotel, the Fleur-de-Lys at Farringforth.'

Mrs Stick could repress her anxiety no longer.

'I couldn't help but catch what you were saying when I came in,' she said.

'What was that, Mrs Stick? Oh yes, murder. I was just telling Mr Rolland that circumstances sometimes lead to it.'

'They do if *you* have anything to do with it,' said Mrs Stick ferociously. 'I knew as soon as this gentleman came to the door what it would mean.'

'Really, Mrs Stick.'

'Well so long as they don't start coming here.'

'Who?'

'Murderers and policemen and that. Mr Gorringer phoned to say he'd be over in a few minutes.' She went out.

This announcement seemed to stir Rolland. He stood up and said: 'I shall see you tomorrow then?'

'Yes. Before lunch.'

Rolland hesitated. Carolus thought he was going to make another reference to fees, but no, he wanted to ask a question.

'What did she mean?' he queried thoughtfully.

'Mrs Stick?'

'Yes. That rigmarole of strange words. What on earth did she mean?'

'Just what she said,' replied Carolus staunchly. *Foie d'agneau pané. Fritots d'endives.* She has her own method of pronunciation. Like Rolland for Rowlands. Or Antoine for Tony Brown. I'll see you tomorrow.'

Three

Carolus, settled snugly into his favourite chair with his whisky-and-soda beside him, was resigned to the imminent arrival of his headmaster.

Mr Gorringer was a large man with vast ears like hairy flappers and protuberant eyes. He enjoyed the pomp of head-mastership, the weighty pronouncements in cliché-ridden prose, the awe in which he believed he was held by his assistants. His life was passed to the band music of his own illusions. He believed he was a figure of consequence in the world, that his wife was a woman of wit, that his school was a famous institution. Only Carolus with his easy flippancy sometimes disturbed his ponderous self-satisfaction. Yet the two men, for different reasons, enjoyed one another's company; Carolus because the headmaster's dialogue and passion for drama delighted him, Mr Gorringer because he secretly enjoyed his occasional part in Carolus's investigations.

He entered, wearing an enormous greatcoat with a fur collar of which Mrs Stick had failed to relieve him in the hall.

'Ah, Deene!' he greeted Carolus heartily. 'January has certainly come in with a cold blast. Mrs Gorringer with one of her happier witticisms, yesterday wished me a *frappé* New Year.'

'Hullo, headmaster. Chuck your coat down there and have a drink.'

With a reproachful glance at Carolus, Mr Gorringer carefully laid his coat across a chair.

'I shall not refuse a little, the merest *soupçon* of whisky,' he announced. Then more solemnly added, 'I had intended to consult you on another matter connected with our syllabus for next term but as I entered, your excellent Mrs Stick whispered in my ear what appeared to be a warning. I gather you are contemplating or already engaged in some activity connected with your unfortunate *penchant* for criminal investigation.'

'What on earth did she say?'

'Her actual words, well meant, no doubt, were scarcely well-chosen. Forgetting my position as your headmaster she spoke as though there was a kind of conspiracy between us. "He's up to something" was what she whispered. I made no reply of course, but I could not but conclude that she alluded to one of these unfortunate criminological diversions of yours.'

'Quite right, headmaster. I leave tomorrow for Farring-forth.'

'Indeed? Not murder, I trust?'

'Not yet,' said Carolus. 'Blackmail. The protection racket.'

Mr Gorringer joined the tips of his fingers.

'I am not so ignorant of the world beyond the confines of our educational backwater that I have failed to see films, originating in the United States of America, which portray those engaged in such activities. But in England, Deene? In this later half of the twentieth century? You can scarcely be serious.'

'Why not? There's plenty of scope in the affluent society.'

'You surely don't intend to involve yourself in anything so

squalid? The investigation of murder I have come, most unwillingly, to accept as a form of recreation in which you indulge during your spare time. But blackmail! It is a most unsuitable preoccupation for a scholar and a gentleman.'

'I have never claimed to be either.'

'You are,' pronounced Mr Gorringer, 'the senior history master at the Queen's School, Newminster. That surely is sufficient.'

Carolus longed to voice a pluralised monosyllable popular during his service in the army, but said only, 'Oh rubbish. I'm a very inquisitive man, that's all.'

Mr Gorringer rose.

'You offend me, Deene. If your position in the school which I have the honour to direct means so little to you that you describe it as "rubbish" I feel I should take my leave.' As though anticipating a protest from Carolus he continued : 'No. No. I am in earnest. The syllabus shall wait until you are in a state of mind to realise its importance.'

Carolus stood up to help him on with his coat, which was not what Mr Gorringer intended.

He turned in the doorway.

'I leave you with some misgivings, Deene. I trust that before we reassemble for the Michaelmas term I shall find you with a better appreciation of the importance of your scholastic duties and free, at least temporarily, of your obsession—yes, sir, obsession—with matters far better left to our excellent police force.'

He strode out and Carolus smiling gently poured himself another drink.

Next day he arrived at the Fleur-de-Lys at Farringforth just as Gloria Gee had taken up her position behind the bar of the

Georgian Lounge. Without seeking Rolland he had entered this carpeted room at once.

Gloria exhibited an expanse of bosom as smooth and tempting as a pink silk cushion. Her hair had an artificial gold sheen, her eyelashes were too long and her ear-rings too heavy—she seemed to have a deplorable tendency to overdo things.

'Goo-ood mor-*ning,*' she called musically, giving Carolus her wide professional smile. 'You're early, aren't you?'

'Used to getting up early in my job,' said Carolus.

'Are you?' She leaned over the bar. 'Let me guess what that is. Meelk Marketing Board? No? News agency? Press, perhaps? Or could it be feelms?'

'Something of that sort,' said Carolus briefly, and realised that the idea of films had a magical effect on Gloria.

He ordered a whisky-and-soda and offered her a drink. Her movements had suddenly taken on an exaggerated gracefulness. She pivoted round to the bottles behind her and held a glass under the bottle measure with fingers delicately extended. Her smile was in slow-motion.

'I'm sure I've seen your face. I expect I ought to know it at once,' she said roguishly to Carolus.

'Not very likely. I'm not a star.'

'Really? Perhaps you direct. I adore the films.'

'You wouldn't if you had to work in them.'

'Oh, but I should. It's what I've always wanted. I have been told...'

'What's wrong with your job here?'

Gloria looked petulant.

'It's all right, I suppose. I *do* meet some interesting people. Tony Curtis came in the other day. But I *don't* think it's what I'm cut out for. Doo yew?'

Carolus appeared to examine her carefully.

'Perhaps not.'

Through the door behind the bar a jolly red-faced man in a chef's white cap emerged, beaming.

'Give us a Guinness, Glor,' he said.

Gloria became very dignified.

'You're not supposed to come into the bar,' she said haughtily.

'What's up with you this morning, sweetheart?'

'Don't call me sweetheart. You can take your Guinness and go back to the kitchen, if you don't mind.'

'Hark at you, Brigitte Bardot.'

Gloria flushed.

'Will you *please* get out?'

The man seemed to realise for the first time that he was interrupting something. His smile faded.

'No need to be nasty,' he said.

'Well, then.'

'I'll see you later. When you've got over it.'

He disappeared and Gloria turned to Carolus.

'You see? They're so *common*.'

'Who was that?' asked Carolus.

'Tom Bridger. He's the assistant *chef*. He's all right, I suppose. But I hate anyone talking like that. It's so silly. That's why I want to get out of here.' She looked fixedly at Carolus. 'I shouldn't care what I did,' she added ambiguously.

'He seemed a nice enough chap,' said Carolus.

'Tom? He's not bad, I suppose, but he shouldn't presume.'

'What's the *chef* like?'

This was not the sort of question Gloria wanted to encourage but she could not avoid answering.

'He's a bit of an old misery,' she said. 'Very good at his job, though. He's jealous of Mr Rolland, I always say. You can tell by the way he talks.'

'I hear there was a scene in the dining-room the other night. A man complaining of food poisoning.'

Gloria gave him a steady look.

'I know nothing about that,' she said curtly.

'You were here at the time, though?'

'In here, yes. I never saw any of it. It wasn't my business.' Or yours, she might have added. To think that she had waited all these years to meet a film director and now that one had come he wanted to talk about the hotel.

'You didn't see the man at all? He didn't come in here for a drink before he went to the dining-room?'

'Whatever do you want to know for?'

'I'm inquisitive.'

'Telling me you are. I thought you were a film director.'

'What's wrong with an inquisitive film director? I like to hear you telling me things. Just ordinary things about your work.'

Gloria recovered.

'Doo yew?'

'Yes. When I asked you about the man with food poisoning you looked quite sulky. Different expression altogether. Almost as though you knew more about it than you wanted to say. Interesting, that.'

'Perhaps I do,' smiled Gloria, registering an impossibly arch expression.

Carolus watched her intently.

'Tell me about it.'

'Well, as a metter of fect he did come in here before dinner,' she said, becoming a mite dramatic and conspiratorial. 'I had quate a long talk with him.'

'What about?'

Arch, again; arch but smiling. She even raised a coy fore-finger.

'That would be telling,' she said.

'Fine, fine,' said Carolus.

'As a metter of fect . . .' Now she was elaborately casual. 'As a matter of fect it was about Imogen Marvell.'

'Go on. *Con brio,*' said Carolus.

'I told him who she is and all about her. He seemed terribly interested. Then I said she was coming on Thursday and he made a little note. That's really all.'

'Good. Now something else.'

Wistfulness replaced the casual expression, wistfulness and sisterly concern.

'Poor Mr Rolland's terribly worried about her visit. After this other episode, I mean. It would be dreadful for the restaur-ant if anything went wrong.'

'Dreadful,' agreed Carolus. 'Have you any reason to sup-pose it will?'

Gloria seemed to wake up.

'I? What do I know about it? It's nothing to do with *me.*'

'One last question. Just stand under that light when you answer it. Good. Now then. Did anyone else speak to the man who complained of food poisoning when he was here?'

Gloria registered deep thought.

'Yes,' she whispered, hanging her head. The answer seemed to have been wrung from her with whips and scorpions.

'Hold it,' said Carolus. 'Who?'

She became in a flash the lady of the underworld with a heart of gold.

'I don't want to get anyone into trouble,' she whispered.

'Go on!' said Carolus enthusiastically.

'Davy Paton. The *chef*'s apprentice. When the man left after shouting at Mr Rolland, Dave Paton followed him out to his car.'

'Relax,' said Carolus. 'Let's have another drink.'

'Was I . . . ? Did I . . . ?'

'You were splendid,' said Carolus, with satisfaction. 'It's not really quite my line. I'm concerned more with actualities. But I'm going to write to Alex Foss.'

'Alex Foss? Will you really?'

Alex Foss was a film producer and an old friend of Carolus. It was characteristic of him that he meant what he said and had not made the girl display her talents merely to gain his own ends.

'I can't promise you anything, Gloria. But Alex will certainly see you.'

'Even if it was only crowd work!' said Gloria ecstatically.

'Well, it's up to you. But he'll see you.'

Carolus found Rolland in his office and guessed that something had happened since yesterday for the man was in a state of white panic.

'Thank God you've come,' he said. 'They rang up last night.'

'They?'

'Rivers. I knew his voice. From a call box. He kept laughing in that frightful way he has.'

'What did he want?'

'To tell me what to do if I changed my mind, he said.'

'What are you to do?'

34

'Put an advert in the Personal Column of the *Daily Post*. "Darling. Am expecting you. Daisy". Then someone will call.'

'And what?'

'It will be a woman. She will come to the bar and have a gin and peppermint. Then she'll ask whether we sell chocolates. I shall have the chocolates locked up in my office and bring a box myself which will contain the notes but be weighted to match a full box. She will pay for them and leave.'

'How will you know it's not some innocent woman asking for chocolates?'

'Because when I'm called, she'll say, "I ought not to eat them really. I'm on a regime."'

'Pretty good. But not cast-iron. If you had told the police beforehand . . .'

'Don't mention the police. These people are dangerous. They would kill me if I went to the police. I know it. That's why I came to you. And for God's sake don't tell anyone I've called you in. It would be nearly as bad. You're going to behave just like everyone else staying here, aren't you?'

'I'll try. I'm not very good at behaving just like everyone else, but I'll try. Did Rivers say any more?'

Rolland fidgeted nervously.

'Yes. They know that Imogen Marvell's coming on Thursday. Rivers seemed to think it was a tremendous joke.'

'I suppose it is—for him. Can't you put her off?'

Rolland stared.

'Put off Imogen Marvell? You must be crazy. I might as well try to put off Judgment Day.'

He shook his head sadly at the wild impossibility of the suggestion.

'Tell me about this young apprentice of yours,' said Carolus.

'Paton? I know very little about him. He came here through an agency.'

'From what background?'

'I have heard since, though it may be nothing but staff gossip, that he has been in an approved school.'

'But there has been no complaint about him here?'

'None from the *chef* under whom he works. I understand that the bar manageress complained of his having been cheeky to her. But that might mean anything or nothing. He seems to be a lively youngster.'

'I see. What about the bar manageress, as you call her. Do any of the men here seem seriously attracted?'

Rolland drummed his fingers on the desk.

'I really don't think you should expect me to indulge in that sort of gossip,' he replied with an attempt at the loftiness of manner he had once shown. 'I have no idea who is attracted to Miss Gee or who finds her *quite* unattractive, as I do.'

'You do?'

'I do. And may I point out that I am deeply concerned with something you almost ignore. On Thursday Imogen Marvell comes here. If these people intend to do it they can ruin my business on that day entirely and for good.'

'That would surely be killing the goose that laid the golden eggs, wouldn't it?'

The metaphor seemed to bring no comfort to Rolland.

Four

On Thursday Carolus rose early because it was a brilliant frosty morning. He occupied a pleasant room on the first floor of the Fleur-de-Lys and from its window he could see the wide space in front of the house and the car park.

There was a bright and busy early morning air about the place, a delivery van or two with cheerful drivers who shouted greetings to Tom Bridger, a whistling youngster delivering newspapers, a crisp atmosphere which promised a clear if chilly day. Carolus decided to pass the morning in complete relaxation in expectation of Imogen Marvell's arrival in the afternoon.

At about four o'clock Carolus woke from a siesta and phoned down for tea. Crossing to the window he looked into the dusk and saw nothing less than the arrival of Imogen Marvell. A pink Rolls-Royce, like a mobile strawberry ice-cream, was driven in and the chauffeur, a handsome young man in a cherry-coloured uniform, jumped out athletically to open the door. From this emerged a drab-looking woman with a shapeless hat and nondescript tweeds who immediately turned towards the car interior as though it were a shrine. It is not easy to get out of a car and be greeted at the same time by those waiting, even when the car is a Rolls with ample door space. There is too often an ungraceful scene with a bottom emerging first or an awkward crablike exit. Imogen Marvell must have practised her movements. She leapt lightly from the car and beamed to Rolland who was standing in the hotel entrance to receive her. Skilled Royalty could not have done it better.

Although the space before the front door was brightly lit, it was impossible from Carolus's window to see more of the women than the dull clothes of the one and the mink coat of the other and he decided to go down to the large chintzy room known as the Residents' Lounge, not to be confused with the Georgian Lounge and Bar. Here he found Miss Marvell enthroned, waiting for the television men to prepare their apparatus, the reporters, who were already in the bar, to encircle her, and any odd bods, like Carolus, to be presented to her.

Beside her like an acolyte squatted her secretary Maud Trudge, a stringy woman who flushed easily and seemed to live in a state of taut anxiety. Her worried expression contrasted, and was intended to contrast, with the serene self-confidence of Imogen Marvell.

Rolland led Carolus to the throne.

'May I introduce Mr Deene, one of our guests?' he asked Imogen Marvell and waited for her smile before announcing her name.

Carolus noticed the woman's voice, evidently trained by a skilled elocutionist.

'How do you do, Mr Deene. Are *you* interested in gastronomy?'

'Not really,' said Carolus. 'I know what I like.'

A condescending smile lit the enamel features.

'Ah. How very English,' she replied. It was evident that she

38

was going to use the occasion for a pronouncement. 'I have nothing against people eating what they like,' she conceded, 'providing that they make some effort to educate the palate. Do you do that, Mr Deene?'

'I'm afraid not. I'm too busy educating my pupils.'

'I see. A schoolmaster,' Miss Marvell said, all interest in her voice dying out as she turned to Rolland.

'I should like to see the *cuisine*,' she announced.

This had evidently been anticipated and a *cortège* moved towards the kitchen in which Carolus took an obscure place. He did not want to miss the scene that would follow.

But here a surprise awaited them and for Rolland it was an unpleasant one. The three members of the kitchen staff were all present, but Antoine instead of wearing a shimmering white uniform and coming forward to greet Miss Marvell was seated in his shirt-sleeves smoking a cigarette and studying the *Evening Standard*. (The crossword, Carolus noted sympathetically.) Tom Bridger's apron was soiled and Davy Paton mechanically swept the floor.

Antoine rose slowly. Carolus saw that he was a dour, cada-verous man.

'This is our *chef-de-cuisine*,' announced Rolland, and then with threatening emphasis, as though Antoine must be made to realise what was happening, 'Miss Imogen Marvell.'

'Afternoon,' said Antoine.

Miss Trudge looked as though her face might disintegrate with anxiety as she watched her employer. But Imogen Mar-vell was equal to the situation.

'How do you do, M'sieur Antoine?' she said. 'I have heard a great deal about you and your *Scampi à la Rolland*.'

'Oh, that,' said Antoine flatly.

'And what are you preparing for us this evening?'

'The usual. Our menu doesn't vary much in winter.'

Some camera flashes, which caused Miss Marvell to adopt her gracious smile, interrupted them. Then she eyed a large drum which had been carelessly left in view.

'I see you use Ova-Crema Liquid Eggifier,' she said.

'Yes,' said Antoine shamelessly.

Miss Marvell, who was a director of the firm manufacturing the product, beamed.

'The best egg-substitute on the market,' she said.

As a piece of dialogue between the *chef* of a restaurant called the Haute Cuisine and the author of a book called *French Cuisine Suprême* this struck Carolus as memorable. But there was more to come.

'And cheese?' asked Imogen Marvell.

'Processo,' said Antoine briefly, indicating another drum.

'Could not be better. It runs so smoothly. What about cooking fat?'

'Been using Lardoline,' said Antoine, 'but I want a change.'

'Try Margolio,' said Imogen Marvell. 'It Fries More Golden,' she added. She was quoting that famous television commercial which showed a triumphant housewife dishing out fried fish in batter to ecstatic children.

The big scene was approaching in which Imogen Marvell was to pin a blue rosette, her own Cordon Bleu, on the breast of a proud Antoine. Miss Trudge stepped forward while Imogen turned to the cameras.

'Haven't you got a *chef*'s uniform?' she whispered to Antoine.

'Only wear it for special occasions,' said Antoine sulkily.

Miss Trudge flushed.

'If *this* is not a special occasion,' she hissed, 'I'd like to know what *is*!'

'Why? Who's she?' asked Antoine.

Miss Trudge would not listen to blasphemy.

'Quick!' she said. 'Put it on!'

'Oh, all right,' said Antoine. 'You'll have to wait then.'

He disappeared and Imogen approached Davy Paton.

'Do you enjoy your work?' she asked.

Davy Paton, a cheerful-looking youth with a sprinkle of humorous freckles, grinned.

'Enjoy it? Good Lord no. It's a frightful bind.'

'You're not *interested* in cooking?'

'I'm giving it a try. If it suits me, I'll go on. If not I'll take something else. D'you like it?'

Imogen Marvell smiled gaily and turned to two reporters.

'An original, evidently. He has just asked *me* if I like cooking!'

She glanced towards Tom Bridger but seemed unwilling to chance her luck further.

Then Antoine returned in a white uniform and under the eye of a television camera the ceremony took place which would enchant several million viewers.

Carolus escaped to the Georgian Lounge and found Gloria Gee at her station.

'Make it a double, Gloria,' he said.

'Isn't she a scream?' said Gloria.

'Your term is more apt than you know. A scream of sheer horror. I wonder where she comes from.'

'Same as me, I shouldn't be surprised. Only she's Got On, hasn't she?'

'She certainly has.'

'Her chauffeur was in just now. I thought he was ever so nice. Dicky Biskett his name is. He says she's an old B.'

'I don't think he exaggerates.'

'He says she's married but hadn't seen her husband for years till he turned up about three months ago. He says he's a funny little man—nothing at all to look at. Well, that's often the way, isn't it? There's a sister, too, he says. She's very nice from what he told me. Not a bit the same style as Her.'

'No?'

'Not by what he says. She's a little dumpy woman who really does know about food and that. It seems She learned it all from her, to start with. Now her sister just manages one of the restaurants.'

'You seem to have had quite a chat.'

'Oh we did. Dicky was telling me . . .'

'Dicky?'

'Dicky Biskett. Her chauffeur. I was telling you about.'

'Oh yes. And what was he telling you?'

'About some of the stars she knows . . .'

They were interrupted by Rolland.

'I want to speak to you,' he said in an urgent low voice. 'I daren't ask you into the office. They would know I'd told you.'

'Come up to my room, Number 8, in five minutes' time,' said Carolus, looking at his grey-tinted skin and agonised eyes.

Rolland went out.

'Whatever's the matter with Mr Rolland?' asked Gloria. 'I expect it's having Her here. She's enough to upset anyone, isn't she?'

Entering Carolus's room with a backward glance as though to see if he were followed, Rolland looked as though he was about to collapse.

'They've come,' he said. 'Rivers and the man he calls Razor Gray.'

'You've seen them?'

'Yes. They came in a big Jaguar.'

'Did you get the registration number this time?'

'Yes,' said Rolland and repeated it. 'They're in the bar now. I know they going to make a scene at dinner.'

'Surely that *is* a matter for the police? If you tell them what they've threatened? At least you can get support if you ask them to leave.'

'I daren't!' said Rolland, a note of hysteria in his voice. 'They'd kill me afterwards. What *am* I to do?'

'Can you rely on your staff?'

'No. You saw this afternoon how Antoine let me down. They're all like that.'

'If you won't call the police and you can't get the help of your staff in ejecting them I don't see what you can do except let things take their course.'

'There is one thing. I could pay.'

'Yes. There is that.'

'Do you advise me to?'

'I can't advise you, Rolland. You must decide for yourself.'

'I won't!' Rolland cried in a high-pitched voice. 'I won't! They would want more and more till everything was gone.'

Carolus shrugged.

'I see your point,' he admitted.

'Can't *you* do anything?' asked Rolland, rounding on Carolus. 'I came to you for help.'

'I warned you that I could do nothing in this situation. I need time in which to observe these people.'

'Oh God!' said Rolland and made for the door. But even now he remembered to be cautious in leaving the room.

When Carolus went down for dinner he was given a table next to that prepared for Imogen Marvell and her secretary. On the other side of it was a table already occupied by two men whom he easily recognised by description as Jimmie Rivers and Razor Gray; the one a beefy brute in a slick expensive suit, the other a taciturn individual less dressy but more dangerous in appearance.

Stefan came for his order. He was an immaculately dressed rather handsome man in his late forties and, in spite of his professional urbanity, Carolus saw that he was drunk. However he began to take his order with automatic politeness.

Carolus ordered an omelette and this produced a blurred protest from Stefan.

'Arent'u go have the *scampi,* sir? Speshalty of the house.'

'No, thank you.'

'Don't blame you,' said Stefan unexpectedly. 'Sick of the bloody things myself.' He pulled himself together. 'I'll send the wine waiter, sir.'

He went away with the deliberate walk of a man controlling himself while intoxicated.

Molt the wine waiter was businesslike and brisk. Also approaching fifty he had greying hair and a plain English face. He took Carolus's order without comment.

Then Imogen Marvell made her entry. It was very splendid, more operatic than theatrical. She advanced to her allotted place with only one indicative gesture from Stefan as though she could not be mistaken about her table, or about anything else. Miss Trudge scurried after her and although Imogen

44

seemed to move with slow deliberation one had the impression that the secretary had to run to keep up with her.

Imogen Marvell sat down and gazed critically around her, examining the other diners as though they were film extras surrounding a star.

Stefan stood slightly behind her while she examined the menu so that she could not see his glazed eyes. But Miss Trudge could and they doubtless added to her anxieties. As Carolus watched he was startled to see Stefan give the secretary a smiling wink which threw Miss Trudge into a turmoil. She flushed to the colour of raw meat and nervously rearranged the silver in front of her.

'Don't fidget, Maud,' said Imogen crisply. Then half turning to Stefan without looking up, she said, 'I . . .' it was an emphatic and long-held monosyllable, 'shall have the *Scampi à la Rolland.*'

'Yes, Miss Marvell,' said Stefan, writing or pretending to write.

'And . . .' She paused before naming the other pretentious dish. 'The *Canard au pamplemousse.*'

'And, madame?' said Stefan as though he had been waiting impatiently for the pleasure of taking Miss Trudge's order.

Miss Trudge flushed again.

'Oh, anything for me.'

'How many times have I told you, Maud, that is no way to treat good food? Or a good *maître d'hôtel,*' she added with a backward smile for Stefan. 'Make up your mind, dear. We haven't got very much time.'

Miss Trudge fumbled wildly with the menu.

'Sole?' she whispered.

45

'Certainly, madame,' said Stefan. 'Sole Royale Montceau. And perhaps *Cailles flambées aux raisins* to follow?'

Miss Trudge nodded hurriedly without realising that she had ordered an elaborate dish of quail which would bring Stefan to the table with a trolley. Perhaps Imogen Marvell did not either, for she made no comment.

But Miss Trudge never ate that quail for after swallowing several of her *scampi,* apparently with relish, Imogen Marvell turned a greenish white and rose uncertainly to her feet.

'Trudge!' she cried. 'Quick! I have been poisoned!'

The diners who were already aware of her identity now stared in wonder. Miss Marvell swayed for a moment then with no attempt at grace or even concealment was violently sick on the floor.

'Call a doctor. Call the police,' she said in a strangled voice. 'Call the proprietor! Disgraceful! I shall sue . . .'

She sat down violently and vomited again. Rolland hurried into the room, Stefan watched blearily and several customers made a hurried exit.

'Scandalous! Abominable!' screeched Imogen Marvell, while Miss Trudge tried to hold her forehead.

Then the most horrifying comment of all was heard for Jimmie Rivers laughed, heartily and long, while Imogen Marvell was carried from the room.

Five

Carolus had been more interested in Rivers and Razor Gray than in the scene at the next table. He had studied the faces of the men as though he meant never to forget a detail of them and followed their reaction to Imogen Marvell's distress. Carolus decided that this had been anticipated by the two, their curiosity aroused only by the form it might take. Perhaps if the famous gastronome had left the room without attracting any attention to herself they were prepared for another kind of action. But the melodrama of Imogen Marvell's departure had exceeded all their expectations.

Carolus left his table inconspicuously and went up to his room. If there had been observers they might have been surprised by the movements of one whom they supposed to be a respectable schoolmaster. He opened his suitcase and took out two souvenirs of the last war, one an American airman's windbreaker designed to give freedom of movement and warmth at the same time, and the other a Nazi souvenir, a genuine rubber truncheon which could render a man insensible without cracking his skull. He put on the windbreaker and concealed the truncheon in it before he left the room.

He went out to the car park and picked out the Jaguar designated by Rolland. He tried the handle and found it was unlocked. Nothing had been left on the seat.

47

Returning to the hotel he found Rolland.

'Switch off the outside lights and keep them off,' he said.

Rolland looked at him tragically.

'What does it matter now?' he asked.

'It matters to me. And to you. Will you make sure the car park lights are left off?'

Rolland nodded and Carolus left him. Then quite unhurriedly he went out to the Jaguar and made himself as comfortable as possible on the floor behind the front seats.

It was not as foolhardy as it appeared. Carolus had noticed how infrequently anyone getting into a car bothers to examine the rear interior, especially when anxious to drive away quickly, and it would need quite careful scrutiny to discover him. He assumed that the car would make for London, a mere thirty miles away. It would be awkward, he owned, if it was to start on an all-night journey to Scotland or Cornwall for even if the two men left the car for a drink or anything else Carolus was determined to remain with it to its destination. This was the only way at present possible to discover more about them.

He calculated his chances of success at something like sixty per cent and knew that failure would be highly dangerous. But there it was. For his own satisfaction he had to do something.

The two men came out of the hotel sooner than Carolus anticipated. Perhaps they felt that their work had been so effectively done for them that they could make for home at once. As they approached the car Carolus heard Razor Gray say curtly 'I'll drive' and knew what he had already suspected —that Gray was, between the two of them, the boss.

They did not speak as they opened doors on both sides and

got in simultaneously without, Carolus could safely deduce, a glance at the back seat of the car. The engine started and Carolus could no longer hear any conversation that may have passed between them.

They seemed to be an eternity in transit and the movements of the car, from where Carolus crouched, were nauseating. He guessed from the growing frequency with which they stopped at traffic lights that they were approaching London. Then there was a halt in which the engine was switched off and Carolus felt sure they had arrived.

'Want me to come up?' asked Rivers.

'No. I'll go. I shan't be long,' Razor replied, and the door slammed.

It was time for action and this would be brief. Carolus pulled out his truncheon. There was a sudden jerk of movement from Rivers—it was evident that he had seen something in the driving mirror—but before he could even turn his head Carolus brought the truncheon down on it and he slumped in his seat.

Carolus felt the pulse and it was beating, though Rivers was unconscious. He had time to dive into the man's breast pocket and remove his wallet. He had planned this because he believed it might contain information or some means of identifying Rivers under his own name. Then he followed the man Razor into the block of flats before which the car was standing. He was amused to think that people had been passing the car throughout this operation.

He saw the name Gaitskell Mansions as he entered the showy entrance hall. He was baffled. There was no sign of Razor Gray and the dial by the door of the lift showed that it was motionless on this floor. He made for the staircase.

'Now, then, now then, where might you be going?'

Carolus turned to see a tall heavy individual with a large well-trained moustache. He was emerging from the concierge's cubby-hole and wore full uniform. Carolus crossed to him.

'Did a man in a grey suit come in just now?'

The concierge whose name was Humbledon had learned in a life dedicated to the collection of gratuities that eager questions led to a sure source of revenue.

'He might have,' he replied.

'Do you know him?'

'I might do,' said Mr Humbledon.

Carolus passed him a fiver.

'What is his name?'

'Ah, I don't know his *name,*' replied the porter, suggesting by his tone that he knew everything else. 'Not his *name* I don't know. But I know him all right. Seen him often.'

'Who does he visit?'

'I don't know whether you would say he visits anyone. Not to say *visit,* that is. He calls to consult Mr Montreith, like a good many others.'

'Who is Mr Montreith?'

'You don't know who Mr Montreith is? I can see you don't know much. Big solicitor. Handles a lot of important business. He has offices on the first floor and lives above them. He's had a staircase made to his flat.'

'Is there another way out of here?' asked Carolus, who had been watching the car and thought he saw signs of movement.

'Only the staff entrance. That gives on Wilsey Place.'

'Show me it, would you?'

He knew it was useless to ask Humbledon for secrecy. Even Razor Gray as he came down in a few minutes would be told, for a tenth of what Carolus had paid, that a man had followed him in and enquired about his movements, and though Humbledon would maintain that he had given no information Gray would read Humbledon at least as well as Carolus had done. The hope, so far as the future was concerned, was that Rivers had not seen enough of him in the driving mirror to recognise him, and that neither of them had reason to connect a man they may have seen dining in the restaurant with anyone at Gaitskell Mansions.

'What street is the front of the building on?' asked Carolus as Humbledon took him to the staff entrance.

'Attlee Avenue,' said Humbledon.

Only when he had walked to the corner and examined the plate giving the street's name did he realise that he was in Bayswater. He went to a phone box and called a Hire Service headquarters for a car to take him back to the Fleur-de-Lys.

Before turning in he left a note asking that copies of all the daily newspapers should be sent up to his room in the morning and after breakfast he lay in bed reading these. He was surprised to find what appeared to be a conspiracy among pressmen to report the incidents of yesterday with a certain slant.

Imogen Marvell had been given her full share of publicity, for she had so exposed her life to public view that details could not be withheld when she provided them, but in such a way that her collapse was the news, not the cause of it or the restaurant where it had happened. 'In one of the restaurants most highly recommended in her *Gourmet's Vade Mecum*, Imogen Marvell . . .' were the opening words of one account, and short of a picture of her in the act of vomiting nothing was spared her of humiliation. The name of the Haute Cuisine was not mentioned but the woman whom one paper called 'the

Grande Gourmette' being carried out of an eating house she had praised just after she had decorated the *chef* with the *cordon bleu* was shown in all its irony.

The explanation lay in the arrogance she had displayed in her dealings with the press. In order to explode this it had been necessary not to identify the place where her fall had been lest an action for libel might lie. Not that the dangerous words 'food poisoning' were ever actually used. The implication was rather that Imogen had been hoist with her own petard.

This would bring small relief to Rolland, Carolus thought. He would still have to face her action for damages if evidence of food poisoning was discovered, and he would still be subject to the dilemma created by Rivers and those he represented. But Imogen Marvell would be enraged.

There was a knock at his door and a little sour-faced woman in an over-all came in with another newspaper. This, he guessed, was Mrs Boot the daily cleaner.

'Here you are. Rolland wanted a read of it first.'

'Thank you,' said Carolus.

'That's just like him. Taking someone else's paper then sending me up all those stairs with it.'

'I'm sorry,' returned Carolus vaguely.

'They'll be the death of me, those stairs. Up and down them fifty times a day. And it's worse with Ur in number four.'

'Do you mean Miss Marvell?' asked Carolus who did not suppose she was referring to the city of the Chaldees.

'Yes. They've put her in there though she hadn't booked. She's making the most of it. I don't know why she wants to make a fuss about a little bit of a turn like that. No one's going to write about it in the papers if I bring up my dinner, are they?'

'I suppose not.'

'Her secretary's been up since eight o'clock telephoning all over the place for doctors and specialists and I don't know what-all. They say her sister has been sent for and her husband has decided to come down this morning. All for a bit of colly-wobbles. Makes you think, doesn't it?'

'Yes,' Carolus admitted.

'I've no use for anything like that,' went on Mrs Boot. 'Not that it doesn't serve that Rolland right. This was a nice quiet pub before he came here. I used to work here in Mistr'an Misses Cheeseman's time and it was very different, I can tell you. No *chefs* and that with French names though they're no more French than what I am. As for that Stefan, as they call him, he's on the booze half the time.'

'You don't seem to care for it much,' said Carolus.

'Can you wonder? What with those two Arabians waiting to stick a knife in you any minute. They give me the creeps— I can tell you that. Did one of them bring your breakfast in this morning?'

'Yes.'

'There. I thought so. People don't like to wake up and find one of those creeping round the room. Then . . .' She paused for breath. 'Then there's Bridger grinning all over his face. What *he* got to grin about I'd like to know, except that he's chasing after that Gloria Gee, as she calls herself. What you say about her, eh? Nice thing to have him waltzing up to her room every night, or so I'm told he does, and it wouldn't surprise me.'

'Don't you approve of anyone, Mrs Boot?'

'Eh? Well, I don't like those that say things behind your back, like Molt does. They call him a wine waiter. I'd like to know what would have been said in Mistr'an Misses Cheese-man's time if anyone had called himself a wine-waiter. Not that *they* were much to write home about. *He* was caught with one of the girls they had working here and *she* had a nasty way of spying on anyone and writing D-U-S-T with her finger on anything there wasn't time to get round to.'

Carolus was determined to break this disapprobationary sequence.

'What about young Davy Paton?' he asked.

'What about him? Thinks too much of himself for my liking. Playing silly jokes half the time. He's another who talks. I've heard what he says about people. I always say if you can't say anything good about anyone don't say anything at all.'

'Very wise.'

'Well I must be getting on otherwise they'll think I don't do my work in the morning.'

She nodded unsmilingly and left Carolus to reconsider her information.

So Imogen was making the most of it. Carolus could imagine her having death-bed scenes and wondered if they would be televised.

He dressed and went downstairs and found Rolland.

'You ought to be pleased,' he said.

'Why?' asked Rolland.

'The press haven't mentioned the name of your restaurant.'

'What good will that do? She's going to sue me.'

'Don't be too sure. It must depend on the medical evidence.'

'Dr Jyves our local man couldn't find anything wrong with her. She raged like a lunatic, called him incompetent and ordered him out of the room. Now she has sent for a specialist.'

'All the same, the first attack was half a failure.'

'They'll soon do something else. Worse probably. I think I shall pay. It's scandalous but you don't seem able to do anything about it. I can't go on like this.'

'I shouldn't do that,' said Carolus. He foresaw an end to the visits of Rivers and the rest and the collapse of his own efforts.

'Why not? Yesterday you wouldn't advise me one way or the other. What makes you tell me not to pay it now?'

He was insistent, looking desperately for some hope.

'I shouldn't. That's all. I can't say much but I have made a start. Hold out as long as you can.'

Rolland was not a fool. Sly, selfish, mean, but quite intelligent.

'Play it off the cuff,' Carolus advised him. 'With any luck they'll give you some breathing space. As for Imogen Marvell, whatever she ate . . .'

'That's just it. She must have been given something. Who do you suppose . . .'

'Whatever she ate she probably brought up when she vomited. The carpet was cleaned at once of course?'

'Of course.'

'Then I doubt if she can prove it was anything she had here.'

'It must have been.'

'Why? But I should take those *scampi* off the menu if I were you.'

'I have,' said Rolland, tragically.

Six

It was clear that Imogen Marvell intended to make her presence felt positively and at every moment of the day. Though reported by Miss Trudge to be remaining in bed 'seriously ill' she succeeded in disturbing the routine of the Fleur-de-Lys and no one, from Antoine to Gloria Gee, was allowed to forget that there was a Very Important Invalid in number four.

Miss Trudge was everywhere. Because it disturbed Imogen to have the telephone in her room used, she hurried about looking distraught and carrying out Imogen's orders.

At ten o'clock arrived the first of those summoned from London to Imogen's bedside. This was her sister Grace Marvell. After a brief interview with the suffering woman, during which she was called elegantly 'a clumsy cow', she was dismissed and came down to the bar for a reviver. Carolus fell into conversation with her.

She was a dumpy, jolly little woman who seemed quite unperturbed by her sister's bad temper and illness.

'Nothing wrong with her,' she confided to Carolus. 'Just tantrums that's all. But that silly old Trudge plays up to her.'

'Miss Trudge is devoted to your sister?'

'A dog-like devotion. Or bitch-like. I can't bear her. Flying about as though she was on fire. Imogen attracts that type, I suppose.'

'Do you share your sister's gastronomic interests, Miss Marvell?'

'I taught her all she knows—which isn't much. It never struck me as important. I knew how to cook but so do millions of women. It took Imogen to turn the knowledge to money.'

'I read a newspaper article of hers in which she spoke of your grandmother, the *Baronne*, from whom she learned the secrets, she said, of the *cuisine française*.'

Grace Marvell grinned.

'Granny was a railway porter's wife who lived in Pimlico. All she could cook was kippers and spuds. It was a joke in the family.'

'It must have been your maternal grandmother,' said Carolus kindly.

'I believe *she* had been connected with catering—as a waitress,' chuckled Grace. 'But Imogen never knew her. She was knocked down by a hansom cab in the Seven Sisters Road and was killed, before Imogen was born. They were both as English as I am and if either of them saw France it was on a day excursion to Boulogne. The *Baronne* is sheer fantasy. But she gets away with it, bless her. She's a phenomenon really.'

Miss Trudge rushed in.

'Oh, Miss Marvell. I've been looking for you. Could you come at once, please? She's asking for you.'

'Cool down, for goodness' sake. I'll come up when I've finished my drink.'

'But she's asking for you!' cried poor Miss Trudge making the nervous movement called wringing the hands.

'All right. All right. Go and tell her I'll be up presently.'

'Oh, I couldn't do that. Won't you *please* come?'

Grace gave Carolus a grin and followed Miss Trudge from the bar.

'It just shows, doesn't it?' commented Gloria.

'It does.'

'Dickie Biskett says those two hate each other now, though they were friendly enough till about three months ago. Jealous, I suppose.'

Yes, thought Carolus. For in spite of her way of discussing her sister one felt that Grace admired her success.

He saw no more of Grace till lunch-time but in the meantime became aware of a vague-looking elderly man who drifted about the Fleur-de-Lys like a stray cat. This, he learned from Gloria, was Imogen's husband. It was typical of him that no one saw him arrive, in fact no one remembered sending for him. He was just there.

Carolus was not very successful in conversation with him. He was courteous, even chatty, but made no reference to The Invalid and could not be led to discuss anything more personal than the weather, the news from Vietnam, the Government and so on. His name, Carolus learned, was Dudley Smithers. Marvell was a professional name which Grace had been obliged to adopt when Imogen became famous. The two sisters were born Grace and Emma Haskins.

'You staying long?' Carolus asked Mr Smithers at the bar.

'No. Not long,' he said. 'It's bracing air down here, though, isn't it? I thought this morning what splendid air this is.'

'You came down last night, perhaps?'

'No. No. I do enjoy a day in the country. Blows the cobwebs away.'

Exasperated Carolus tried a direct attack.

'How is Miss Marvell this morning?' he asked.

'She's doing nicely,' said Mr Smithers. Then, chirpily he asked: 'Are you staying in the hotel?'

Carolus, temporarily defeated, decided to retire.

In the hall he found a curious little scene in progress. An impressive-looking elderly man was speaking in a loud but cultured voice to Miss Trudge who with scarlet face positively writhed before him.

'You told me on the telephone it was a case of life and death,' he said. 'I've wasted an entire morning coming down here.'

'Your fee will be paid, Sir Glynn,' said poor Miss Trudge reproachfully.

'Fee? Do you think I'm talking about fees? I have several important cases in the hospital, people who need attention, and you bring me down to see a hysterical woman with a small bilious attack, and *that* induced by her own self-pity.'

'Oh, Sir Glynn! How can you speak like that? Miss Marvell is seriously ill. You haven't even prescribed anything for her!'

'I'll prescribe. One mile's walk a day to be increased, by extending it daily, to five miles. Cut out all animal fats, all farinaceous food and all sugar. Give her a dose of castor oil immediately. And never call me down on what I can only describe as a wild GOOSE chase!'

He nodded briskly and went out. His car was chauffeur-driven and carried him away smoothly. Miss Trudge was in tears.

'I was told he was the *best* specialist for this trouble,' she appealed to Carolus. 'You heard him? How could he speak like that?'

'I don't imagine Miss Marvell will be very pleased with his advice.'

'I should not dream of telling her,' said Miss Trudge, with an anxious glance upward towards the room in which The Invalid lay.

But she must have given Imogen some indication of the specialist's advice for as Carolus passed her door later he heard a scream of fury.

He paused there for a moment—it could scarcely be called eavesdropping because Imogen's voice rang through the house.

'I shall expose him!' she cried. 'Exercise! No sugar! Castor oil! The man must be a charlatan. Trudge! Do you hear? I shall expose him. Is there no one I can depend on? Where's my sister? Gone in to *lunch*? How dare she when I can eat nothing. Fetch her at once. At once, do you hear? And Rolland! And get another doctor! Phone immediately. Say that Imogen Marvell needs attention. Move, woman! The man's a scoundrel. Five miles a day! No animal fats! He must be mad. It's a conspiracy! I'm surrounded with jealousy. If you don't move, Trudge, I shall get out of bed and shake you!'

Miss Trudge came out, a strange pallor taking the place of her usual crimson. She bolted downstairs. It was in fact pleasant for Carolus to observe at lunch-time the tranquil calm with which Imogen's self-effacing husband, Dudley Smithers, ate his way through several courses. Perhaps he knew Imogen better than any of them.

Then at something past four in the afternoon, Carolus did that thing dear to the heart of English hotel residents, he 'had tea in the lounge'.

Miss Trudge was there swallowing a hasty cuppa because she had not been able to come down to lunch. Carolus asked earnestly after Imogen Marvell.

'She is very brave,' said Miss Trudge somewhat ambiguously. 'But unfortunately she insists on looking at the daily newspapers. I have kept them from her till now but as soon as she finishes her nap she is determined to see them. I'm afraid it will cause a relapse.'

'What form is that likely to take?'

'She is so sensitive. She will be deeply hurt by the way the story has been interpreted. It will send her temperature up, I'm afraid. It's so bad for her to become excited. I think I'll run and see if she has woken up.'

She meant it literally. Her exit was at the double.

Half an hour later Grace Marvell walked in chuckling.

'She's screaming blue murder,' she said. 'She's been looking at her press.'

'Not very comforting, I'm afraid,' said Carolus.

Grace smiled.

'She's in hysterics. What's more she can keep this up till tomorrow morning. I've known her scream her head off for hours at a stretch if things go against her. It's frustrating, of course. She'll have to be given an injection presently to make her sleep, otherwise the whole hotel will be disturbed.'

'You seem to know her very well.'

'I ought to. I was brought up with her. She was the only girl at school who could get her way with the headmistress— one of those granite women—by simply screaming till she did.'

Miss Trudge dashed in.

'She wants Mr Smithers!' she cried. 'We shall have to get another doctor for her!'

She hurried off.

'She means Imogen's husband,' explained Grace.

'Surely he has a calming effect?'

'Oh, no. His coolness drives her insane. He doesn't blink an eyelid while she abuses him with every insult under the sun. It's harrowing to see them together.'

'Why does he put up with it?'

'Imogen's enormously rich,' Grace explained adequately. 'Though I don't see what *he* can hope for.'

Carolus was glad to escape from this atmosphere when he made for the bar soon after six o'clock.

He thought Gloria looked a little sulky at first and mentioned that he had written a note to his friend Alex Foss which seemed to cheer her up.

'Have you really?' she said. 'That's ever so nice of you.'

For a few minutes she was absent-minded as though away in a dream world of her own. But she returned to give him some surprising news.

'Who do you think booked in just now? Staying the night.'

'Who?' asked Carolus obligingly.

'The man I told you about! The one who made the scene about food poisoning the *other* time. You remember? I said he came in here and had quate a chet with me.'

'Yes, indeed.'

'Well, he's come back. I shouldn't have thought he would after what happened, would you?'

They were interrupted by the entrance of an individual of sanguine complexion in a check suit. Behind his back Gloria made excited signals to Carolus to indicate that it was the man they had been discussing. He ordered vodka-and-tonic and sat beside Carolus. He seemed anxious for conversation so having agreed that it was a dirty night and the Government was hell, Carolus asked him if he often came here.

'Not more than I can help. Last time I was here I got food poisoning. I'm deciding whether to bring an action for damages, or not. Since I read of the same thing happening to this cookbook woman, I feel something should be done.'

Carolus thought Imogen's health might not improve if she heard herself called 'this cookbook woman.'

'So you're going to try the food again? That's very courageous of you.'

'I'm going to see the proprietor, or whatever he is.'

Carolus studied the man narrowly. Was he or was he not connected with Rivers and the rest?

'Live in London?' Carolus queried in a tone of idle chatter.

'Yes. I'd move out myself but the wife won't live anywhere else. Do you?'

'Bayswater,' said Carolus quickly.

Yes. It had struck home. With tremendous casualness the man asked: 'What part of Bayswater?'

'Wilsey Place,' said Carolus. He did not mean to commit himself too far.

So pointedly lacking in interest was the man that Carolus felt fairly certain of him.

'Hm? Don't know that part. Live in Chelsea myself. Have a drink?'

'Thanks.'

'Must have been quite a *thing,* this diet expert passing out.'

'It was. Hope you had nothing like that?'

'It was very unpleasant. Very unpleasant. Ought to be more careful in a restaurant like this.'

Rolland entered.

'Ah, there you are, Rolland,' said the stranger, his manner becoming rather aggressive. 'I wanted a word with you.'

Rolland's attempt at dignity was pitiable. His nerve had evidently broken down.

63

'I've nothing to say to you,' he said. 'You had better get in touch with my solicitors.'

'*I* get in touch with *your* solicitors? That's a laugh. I'll sue you for every penny you've got. I came here to speak to you in private on this matter before going for you with the utmost rigour of the law.'

Rolland hesitated.

'I suppose you had better come to my office,' he said wearily and the two men went out.

'Poor Mr Rolland,' said Gloria. 'He must be out of his mind with all this happening and Her upstairs. You'd think Antoine could tell good *scampi* from bad, wouldn't you? It's beyond me, I must say.'

Seven

Miss Trudge rushed in.

'Is Mr Smithers here?' she asked.

It was perfectly obvious that he was not, but Miss Trudge looked about her rather wildly.

'May I offer you a drink, Miss Trudge?' asked Carolus.

Miss Trudge stopped fidgeting sufficiently to give Carolus a hurried smile.

'Oh, I couldn't possibly,' she said with emphasis. 'It would not be . . . With Imogen in bed . . . It's very kind . . . It might be perceptible when I am near her, you see . . . It has been rather a trying day . . . So kind of you to think . . . Perhaps a teeny brandy then, but I must get back . . .'

She sipped gratefully but as she raised her arm Carolus saw that there was blood at her wrist. She tried to cover this, and he felt it better to say nothing.

Just then Grace Marvell came in.

'You're smothered in blood,' she said to Miss Trudge. 'Whatever's the matter? Look at your arm! Wait—let me look.'

Her examination revealed a long scratch from near the elbow.

'You're an idiot, really you are. This might turn to blood-poisoning. You deserve it for the way you allow that sister of mine to walk over you. But we can't have any more scandal. I'll have to do it up. Is there a chemist's near here?'

'Mr Fulbright,' said Gloria. 'Just down the road. You remember. You bought the eau-de-cologne there this afternoon.'

'Oh, yes. I'll go and get some plaster. You're a nuisance but that could be serious if it's not attended to. Imogen's fingers must be tipped with poison. Stay here.'

She went out by the street entrance of the bar.

'It's a nasty scratch,' said Gloria. 'However did you get it?'

Not tactful, Carolus thought. Miss Trudge writhed.

'It's nothing, really. Just a little . . . scratch. Miss Marvell needn't have bothered. Must have been my brooch . . .'

'Your brooch? But how . . .' began Gloria till she caught Carolus's discouraging eye.

Grace returned.

'Come on,' she said briskly to Miss Trudge. 'The chemist was just closing but I managed to get some alcohol and plaster.'

They went out.

'She's really very kind,' commented Gloria. 'Only it's her manner. I'm sorry for Miss Trudge, though. I suppose it was that Imogen who scratched her arm?'

Presently Miss Trudge returned.

'I don't think I quite finished my . . .' She blushed violently. 'No, there it is . . . So kind . . .'

'Have another?' said Carolus.

'You *are* kind . . . I wonder whether . . . just for once . . . it's not as though I . . . She told me not to come back for half an hour . . .'

Evidently the brandy was what is called 'doing her good'.

But Grace Marvell when she came in was in a very downright mood.

'We must phone the local doctor,' she said. 'He'll have to give her a shot of something to put her out for a few hours. She'll have convulsions if he doesn't. I don't mind her yelling at me but this has gone past all bounds. You know the doctor's number, Trudge. Get him round here as soon as possible.'

'You really think?'

'Certain. It's the only thing to do. She'll burst a blood vessel.'

'She may not like having an injection . . .'

'I don't suppose she will. But it's for her own good. You don't know what she's like in this condition.'

'If you're sure it's the right thing,' Miss Trudge said dubiously.

'Go and phone!' retorted Grace and Miss Trudge went. A few minutes later Grace followed her out.

'It's not the first time,' said Gloria. 'Dickie Biskett was telling me they had the same thing with her about three months ago. Then it was about a recipe she had written in a newspaper. She'd said *two hours* in the oven by mistake and people were writing in from everywhere saying it was burnt to a cinder. They had her London doctor then and he put her to sleep.'

'Your friend's very informative. You seem to get on with him.'

Gloria jerked her head back.

'He thinks too much of himself,' she said. 'I don't like anyone who presumes.'

Carolus went into the dining-room for dinner and looked about him. There was plenty to observe. The florid man was dining alone and apparently enjoying his food. He made no attempt to disturb the other diners of whom there were perhaps two dozen. At the table occupied previously by Imogen Marvell, her sister and husband sat facing one another and eating in silence. Stefan seemed sober and there was no sign of Miss Trudge.

He was surprised at the quiet behaviour of the florid man, who had almost finished his dinner. Had Rolland capitulated?

Miss Trudge came in and spoke to Grace Marvell.

'The doctor's coming at nine o'clock,' she said.

'Good.'

'I must get back to her.'

Mr Smithers gave no sign of interest, but continued to masticate complacently.

Looking back on that evening and the night that followed Carolus thought that events moved with a certain crescendo from the arrival of Miss Trudge with a scratched arm to the moment when death was discovered.

There was first of all the appearance of Dr Jyves. Carolus was sitting alone in the Residents' Lounge when Grace Marvell came in with a small dusty-looking man in a soiled raincoat. He carried a bag and his face twitched at intervals. Cocaine, Carolus decided.

Either the two of them did not know Carolus was there, or their business was so urgent that they decided to ignore him.

'She needs an injection. If she's not put to sleep at once she'll drive us all mad. Miss Trudge, her secretary, is nearly out of her mind already.'

'I'll see her at once,' said the doctor, twitching violently.

'What will you give her? Dormodina?'

'If it's necessary.'

'It is necessary. She's been hysterical all day. We've had this before, doctor, when she doesn't get her own way. Her own doctor injected Dormodina. She was all right next morning.'

'Very well. Let me see her,' said Dr Jyves.

They went out, leaving the door open, and Carolus heard them going upstairs.

It was a quarter of an hour at least before Grace Marvell returned and spoke to Carolus.

'Out like a light,' she said cheerfully. 'It's the only way when she's like that. We had a terrible job to persuade her to take the injection. I nearly told her it was that or a strait-jacket. But in the end we persuaded her.'

'And you think she will have recovered by the morning?'

'Oh, yes. The next act will be a wistful one. Alone in the world. No one cares whether I live or die. Then she'll pack up and return to London and give hell to her staff and if he's any-where about to her husband.'

'Mr Smithers seems quite unperturbed by it all,' observed Carolus.

Grace did not seem to find this an impertinent remark from a stranger.

'He's a funny little man. No one knows what he does think. He came down of his own accord after he had read in the papers about her collapse. They haven't lived together for ten years, you know.'

She rang the bell and, when one of the two Moroccans appeared, ordered coffee. She seemed ready to go on chatting with Carolus.

'A funny thing happened upstairs just now,' she said. 'You noticed that rather beefy looking man who dined alone this evening, at the table next to ours? He's staying in the hotel, I think.'

'Yes?' said Carolus encouragingly.

'He seemed to be waiting on the landing when I came out of Imogen's room with the doctor. He stopped us and asked how she was. I told him she had just had an injection and was sleeping soundly. He said, "That's good. We shall all get some sleep now." I thought it was rather cheek but I suppose she *has* been making rather a noise.'

'Is his room near hers?'

'He didn't say. I suppose he's on the same floor. I think the top floor is only for the staff.'

'There are some staff quarters across the yard, though,' said Carolus.

'Oh, are there? I really don't know. I shall be glad to get back to my own flat, anyway. I hope my sister's better to-morrow.'

At twenty past ten Miss Trudge appeared.

'I sat with her for a time,' she said, 'but she is sleeping so peacefully now that I felt I could leave her.'

She spoke as much to Carolus as to Grace. He gathered that the two women communicated only when it was necessary.

Miss Trudge sighed.

'It's been *such* a day,' she said.

'What you need, what we all need, is a drink,' said Carolus confidently. 'Let me . . .'

He rang the bell.

'Oh no,' said Miss Trudge. 'You are really *too* kind . . . I don't feel I should . . . Perhaps the weeniest . . . I do feel a little exhausted.'

'You, Miss Marvell?'

'Cointreau,' said Grace briefly.

Carolus ordered three doubles. He had stayed in the Residents' Lounge too long.

'I wonder where Mr Smithers is,' said Miss Trudge. 'I think I ought to warn him that she is sleeping in case he should look in.'

'Don't bother,' said Grace. 'Nothing would wake her.'

'I think I really ought . . . Perhaps he is in the bar. I'll just run and see. In case.'

She was gone for about ten minutes.

'Yes, he did happen to be in the bar. Talking to another gentleman. The one who is staying here. I told him Imogen was fast asleep.'

'What did he say?'

'You know him. He scarcely seemed to notice what I said at first. Then he asked me if I was going to sit up with her.'

'What nonsense!' said Grace. 'Sit up with her? Whatever for? She'll sleep like a log all night. You go to bed. You've got tomorrow to face.'

'But I think I should be near her,' said Miss Trudge. 'Suppose she wakes up and wants something.'

'You're in the next room.'

'I scarcely know what to do for the best. I really am rather exhausted, but she might not like it if I left her on her own.'

'She won't know. You can go in in the morning. For goodness' sake stop being tragic about it. She's got a constitution like a horse.'

'But if she were to wake . . . alone . . . However, I shall be next door, after all. Perhaps I might take advantage . . . a sleep certainly will be welcome.'

Grace gave an exasperated sigh but said no more.

When Carolus reached his room at something past eleven he

found Rolland waiting for him there. The proprietor made desperate signals for silence then spoke in a voice scarcely above a whisper.

'I had to see you. Daren't ask you to the office.'

'That's all right. What is it now?'

'Rivers was on the phone again. Offering me yet another chance. I said they had done all they could and the business was ruined. He laughed, of course. "All we can?" he said. "We're only just starting." '

'What was the particular threat this time?'

'He didn't say at first. He said they were making it easy for me. They had their representative on the spot.'

'The man who made the fuss the other night?'

'Yes. His name's Mandeville, apparently. If I decide to "employ" them, as Rivers calls it, I must see him. Only he has had to put the price up, he says. Expenses and delay. They now want £1250.'

'You mean he admitted that he was part of their organisation?'

'Yes. It seems a most extraordinary thing that they should work in this blatant way. They threaten quite openly. They must be very sure of themselves.'

'So long as you don't go to the law obviously *they* won't. They wanted you to hand £1250 to the man they call Mandeville. When?'

'This evening, presumably. I don't know whether they think I keep that sort of money in the till.'

'I expect they thought you had it ready. And if not?'

'If not Rivers found this very funny—disasters never come at once. Only this time it would be more serious. I asked what he meant and he said, *really* serious. "Life and death sort of thing," he said. Then added, "Yes, death. You know what death is?" I asked him whose death but he only laughed again.'

'So once again you refused?'

'Yes. £1250 is a lot of money. And how could I account for it in income tax returns? I refused but I don't know how long I can hold out. It's bad enough to have Imogen Marvell in hysterics. Saying I was a cook in the army.'

'And were you?'

'Officers' Mess,' said Rolland briefly. 'She's a dreadful woman. I wish she was dead.'

'She may be,' said Carolus quietly.

Rolland jumped up.

'What?' he said, forgetting to keep his voice down.

'She has enemies enough,' explained Carolus.

Rolland very cautiously began to move towards the door.

'Which room is Mandeville in?'

'Six. On this floor.'

'What about the floor above?'

'All single rooms.'

'Any of the staff sleep there?'

'Only the bar manageress. The men have quarters across the yard.'

He began to open the door very cautiously peering out. Suddenly he drew back like a tortoise and shut the door. The two men waited without speaking while footsteps went by.

'Bridger,' explained Rolland. 'Coming down from the floor above. I don't think he saw me.'

He seemed unduly agitated. 'There's only Gloria up there. He must have been with her.' The officious hotel proprietor of other days seemed to awaken in him. 'I *won't* have that. It's forbidden for any of the male staff to go up there. I shall deal with this in the morning.'

'Haven't you got other things to think about?'

'I won't have it,' he said but with less resolution, then again opened the door and with great caution slipped out.

But Carolus did not go to bed. He sat motionless in an armchair, not even smoking. The house was centrally heated and it was a fad of his to detest this. But it was not only the stuffy atmosphere which troubled him. Something was very much amiss here, something more than the blackmailing of Rolland. He went over scraps of talk he had heard that day, trying to find pieces of the jigsaw which puzzled him. Perhaps it was an instinctive sense of apprehension. He was supposed to have instincts which warned him of violence, cruelty, horror, death before any of them were evident to others.

Then, at some time after one o'clock, he suddenly grew alert and strained to listen. Yes, footsteps again and this time cautious ones.

He crossed to the door and did as Rolland had done, opened it silently and no more than a crack. He heard the footsteps going towards the head of the wide stairway which went down to the hall. Only at the moment when whoever had passed was descending the first stairs did he open his door enough to recognise him by the dim landing light. It was the man known as Mandeville and he carried a small suitcase.

Carolus closed his door, switched off the light and went to the window. As he expected, after a few moments he heard the front door being opened and though he could see almost nothing in the darkness he felt sure that the man had gone out.

He waited. There was no moon and the night was black and

still but once he heard footsteps on the gravel and gathered that Mandeville was making for the road.

Nothing was moving. No sound came from the hotel or from the night about him. Traffic had ceased and there was not even the bark of a dog.

Then a car approached. He could see its headlights at some distance. He waited expectantly and sure enough it stopped, not within his range of vision but a few yards from the front of the hotel. Its door slammed and it drove on, past the hotel, on the road to London.

'Nice timing,' thought Carolus. Looking at his watch he saw it was one thirty-one.

Eight

Carolus was awakened by Mrs Boot.

'She's dead,' she announced.

Carolus sat up abruptly.

'Who's dead?' he asked obligingly though there was little need for the question.

'Ur, in number four, the cookery book woman.'

'How do you know?'

'How do I know? With the doctor examining her and the secretary in hysterics and her sister sending for the police . . .'

'Why the police?'

'She'd been murdered, hadn't she?' asked Mrs Boot. 'At least that's what it looks like to me. Suffocation, they call it, while she was sleeping off that injection the doctor gave her, but I'd call it something else. Well, I told them. You can't go on speaking evil about people without something happening. And look at her husband! Creeping round like a cat. A lot he cared when she was taken bad. Nor her sister either. It wasn't natural. Not when anyone might be dying for all they knew.

'There isn't one of them that may not have done it,' went on Mrs Boot rapturously. 'I wouldn't put it past a single one. All they had to do was strangle her while she was asleep.'

'That would leave evidence,' pointed out Carolus.

'Who's to say there isn't? And proof too, if it comes to that.

What about those Arabians? They could have slinked up, slipped in and squeezed the life out of her in next to no time, couldn't they? And you can't tell me they're not the right ones for the job. You've only got to see the way they pick up a knife to know what they are.'

'But what motive would they have?' asked Carolus patiently.

'Who's to say with foreigners like that? It's a good job we haven't all been strangled. Then what about her sister? Or her secretary, if it comes to that? They say she'd got plenty of money and there's no telling what people will do for that. What's more there was a man staying in number six last night who's gone off without paying his bill. Must have got up before it was light and crept off without anyone seeing him. What d'you say to that?'

'Nothing,' Carolus replied meekly.

'The boss caught that Bridger over here last night. What was he doing, I should like to know!'

'I could tell you,' said Carolus.

'Now. Now. I didn't ask for any vulgarity. He had only to nip into her room on the way out and suffocate her without a soul being the wiser. Or that Stefan hadn't done it. There isn't one of them you can trust. As for Antoine, what was to stop him? The apprentice is a little fiend, too. But it's not to say it was a man. A woman could have done it just as easily and that Gloria was on the spot, as you might say.'

'What about me?' asked Carolus, seeing she was running out of possibilities.

'Well,' considered Mrs Boot. 'I'm not saying anything. I hope you'd be too much of a gentleman for anything like that, but who's to say what might come over anyone when you think of the way she behaved. Well, she's gone now, whoever it was, and the whole place upside down. I suppose we shall have a inquest.'

When Carolus came downstairs he found things a good deal more calm than Mrs Boot had led him to expect. Imogen was dead but there was no reason to suppose that she had not died by the unfortunate accident of turning on her face while unconscious and being suffocated—an outcome of the very heavy sleep induced by the injection of Dormodina. Such at least was the opinion of Dr Jyves, Carolus was told.

It was true that Miss Trudge had behaved somewhat melodramatically when she made the discovery in the early morning and had seemed almost as convinced as Mrs Boot that someone was responsible, if only herself for leaving her or the doctor for giving her an injection. But she had locked herself in her room now, and could be heard weeping.

Grace Marvell, predictably, was calmer about it but it seemed that she too was deeply affected. The staff, for the most part, behaved with discretion and the routine of the hotel continued. At first, at any rate, Imogen caused less sensation dead than alive.

Carolus had no wish to view the body having little faith in information gained from cigarette ash, fluff on the hair, footmarks on the carpet, the old-fashioned clues of fictional detectives, but confident that medical evidence, when it was forthcoming, would establish the cause of death. He had reason to regret this later.

He found Grace Marvell when he met her in the Georgian Lounge as down-to-earth as he expected, though there were signs of strain in her manner.

'I don't blame Jyves,' she said. 'She needed something pretty potent to put her to sleep in her condition of last night. But

I gather there have been other accidents of this kind in heavy drug-induced sleep. People have been known to swallow their tongues.'

'You feel sure it was an accident?'

'Oh, yes. Poor Imogen was a woman who made plenty of people say "I could murder Imogen Marvell!" but the mere fact that they said it meant that they never contemplated anything of the sort. There could be no motive, really. Besides, it would be obvious, wouldn't it?'

'I should have thought not necessarily,' said Carolus.

'Anyhow, there's to be an inquest at which we shall hear all the evidence. I'm not quite sure whether Imogen would have liked that or not. It will certainly make headlines.'

It did. During the days that followed Imogen Marvell's name appeared in type as large as had been accorded her in her life-time. But the coroner's verdict was disappointing for those who had expected more startling developments. She had died, it was found, as the result of an accident. There was the merest suggestion of censure for Dr Jyves who made an unfortunate impression when he gave evidence, but none for Miss Trudge who tried to accuse herself of negligence in not staying with Imogen that night.

Only one point emerged from the expert medical evidence. The doctors agreed in thinking that death had occurred at some time in the evening, probably before eleven o'clock. This seemed to surprise most of those who attended the inquest since for some reason it had been thought that a death of that sort would have been likelier in the small hours when resistance was at its lowest. But there were no other surprises and members of the staff who gave evidence added little or nothing to the coroner's information.

Even so, and in spite of the clear-cut medical evidence, an impression was left in the public mind that something was unrevealed. This was interpreted by Mrs Boot in conversation with Carolus.

'An accident!' she said witheringly. 'What kind of an accident is it when a woman in the prime of her life pops off in the middle of the night just because she's sleeping heavy? There's something they're hushing up, you can be sure of that.'

Mrs Boot used the indefinite 'they' with great effect.

'You think so, Mrs Boot?'

'*Course* there is. Stands to reason, doesn't it? *She* had no wish to go, making all that money and her picture in the papers all the time. A big strong woman like that. You can't tell me she just put her head in the pillows and snuffed it. Nor don't a lot of other people think so, either. It looks fishy to me and I've said so all along. With that money, too.'

'What money?'

'Well, she had money, didn't she? You couldn't carry on like that for nothing. Where there's a lot of money there's them that wish anyone out of the way. That's what I say. You wait and see who's going to get it, then you'll know something. You'd think the police would see that, instead of believing every word those doctors said. I don't like doctors, myself.'

'Homoeopathic?'

'Certainly not. I don't believe in anything unnatural. But when a doctor tells me something I do the opposite and ten to one it cures me. Look at my varicose veins.' The invitation, fortunately, was metaphorical. 'Suppose I'd done what the doctor told me, I'd of been as good as crippled for life. You take my word for it, doctors are dangerous. Saying it was an accident! How do *they* know? Anyone could have walked in and done for her before she could holler out. I'd like to know who *did* go to her room that night.'

'So would I,' admitted Carolus.

'We haven't heard the last of it, that's one certainty. What about the man who went off without paying his bill? They didn't get him to the inquest, did they?'

'No.'

'I could have told them something about him,' said Mrs Boot triumphantly. '*They* think he only arrived here in time for dinner that night. I could tell them different. What was he doing in the Spinning Wheel Café that afternoon I'd like to know.'

'Having tea, probably.'

'Certainly he was having tea. But *who with*? That's where it comes in. And don't say he wasn't because I saw him with my own eyes when I went in to get a currant loaf which my husband will have for his tea though the baker doesn't sell them.'

'You saw him? How do you know it was the man who went off without paying his bill?'

'It was the same who made all the fuss a week ago, before this all happened. Wasn't I helping in the kitchen that evening, as I always do Thursdays when it's the boy's night off. "Oh," I thought when I saw him. "So you're back again. That'll mean trouble," I thought.'

'You said he was with someone in the café.'

'So he was. What's more, you'd be surprised to know who it was.'

'I don't think I should. Tom Bridger?'

Mrs Boot looked disappointed. She had expected to surprise Carolus.

'I don't know what makes you come out with that,' she said.

'Unless you're mixed up in it, too. But that's who it was, as large as life. I never liked that Bridger. You can't trust people who are always smiling. There he was talking away to this man. He tried to pass it off, of course. "Afternoon, Mrs Boot," he said when he saw I'd seen him. But that wouldn't do for me. I gave him a look he won't forget in a hurry. "Afternoon," I said and walked out. It isn't as though he couldn't have had his tea here, either. I suppose they had to meet somewhere where no one would recognise them and thought they would be safe there. They was right inside the café where no one could see them from the shop only I just happened to look in while I was waiting for my change.'

'They might have met by chance,' said Carolus.

'You can *say* that,' conceded Mrs Boot. 'But who's going to believe you? I know better, anyway. I said to Tom Bridger, "Wasn't that the man who made all the fuss about his dinner I saw you with in the Spinning Wheel?" I said. He laughed like he always does and said he'd never seen the man before in his life. But there you are. It had Something To Do With It, I'm sure of that. Well, I must be getting on.'

Getting on, where? Carolus wondered. Getting on to what? In that world of dark suspicions and hard thoughts of everyone which Mrs Boot created around herself, she must surely stand alone like a spire surrounded with wheeling black bats. Who escaped her evil-minded conjectures? Perhaps her husband?

'Does your husband work near here, Mrs Boot?'

'No. He doesn't. He works for the Council. Otherwise he'd know everything about it, same as he always does. Oh, yes. He'd know. I often wonder if there's anything he doesn't know. I asked him the other night. "What don't you know?" I said.'

'What did he say?'

'He didn't know what to say. It's the same with his sister. Only she never knows anything good about anyone. You'd think we were all criminals the way she talks. I don't believe in that. You've got to think the best of people, I always tell her. Unless they go saying nasty things behind anyone's back. Well, this won't do. I can't stop listening to you all day when I've got my work.'

Mrs Boot made no move towards departure, however.

'I'll tell you another thing which makes me think,' she offered. 'No one thought to ask where those two Arabians were that night, did they? Well, I could have told them. As soon as I got here on the morning the woman in number four was found dead, Mr Rolland sent me over to fetch them because they ought to have been down for an hour or more and he wanted to send them somewhere. So I went over to where the staff lives and what do you think I found in their room?'

'I have no idea,' said Carolus encouragingly.

'Nothing!' It was a cry of triumph. 'No one. The beds had never been slept in. I thought to myself, they've gone. Hopped it, I thought. Not that I was surprised. You can never tell with anyone like that. They're not the same as you'n me. It would have been nothing for them to go off in the night. Just as I was going back to tell Mr Rolland one of them came in and was quite nasty. "Why you here?" he asks and looks at me like a savage. I wouldn't demean myself arguing. I said, "Mr Rolland wants you quick," I said, and came away. I didn't fancy being up there with him. Then the other came in and they started talking heathen.'

'No. Arabic.'

'I don't know what it was but they sounded as though they

were clearing their throats. What do you think of that? They didn't know *that* at the inquest, did they? Well, I must make a move. My work's not going to do itself, is it?'

Carolus learned that the body of Imogen Marvell was to be taken from the Fleur-de-Lys, 'her favourite hotel' it came to be designated in the press, to be buried in the local churchyard. It seemed that Rolland had decided that the great disaster that had come to him might yet be turned to his advantage and he had persuaded Grace Marvell and Imogen's husband that the publicity which this would bring him would be only fair recompense for what he had suffered. The food poisoning angle was forgotten and Imogen had died from another cause while paying her annual visit to the hostelry where she was most at home, to whose restaurant she had awarded the coveted five stars.

Preparations went forward on a lavish scale. The coffin was to be followed by a retinue of discreet Rolls-Royce and Daimler cars in the first of which her husband, her sister and Miss Trudge were to travel. They were to be followed by three cars in which the *chefs de cuisine* of famous restaurants would ride and the funeral would be attended by a concourse of *restaurateurs,* writers on food and wine, PROs, members of editorial staffs, pressmen, wine-merchants and professional *gourmets*. It had been suggested that a funeral oration should be delivered by the famous author of several expensive coffee-table cookery books but Grace Marvell had put her foot down there.

Carolus waited with cynical curiosity for the occasion and when it came was not surprised to see that on the coffin was laid a rosette larger than any wreath elaborately made up of twelve-inch-wide blue ribbon, the proud symbol of *cordon bleu*. Rolland had given orders for it.

Nine

Carolus realised with a disturbing jerk that only ten days of the school holiday remained and that if he were to learn the truth about events at the Fleur-de-Lys and the death of Imogen Marvell and the firm of solicitors in Gaitskell Mansions he would have to move quickly. Yet his habits could not be broken and he methodically set about the questioning of people concerned.

He was aware that every movement of everyone in the hotel, including the staff, was known to everyone else and to conduct the interviews he wanted was no easy matter. He had some questions for Dave Paton, the apprentice, for example.

Gloria solved that one.

'I'll tell him to go up to your room when he finishes work,' she said. 'That'll be soon after closing time.'

When the youth sloped in it was obvious that he had misunderstood the motive of the summons.

'I can't stay long,' he said.

'That's all right. I just want to ask you a few questions.'

'Aren't you going to offer me a drink first?'

'And call one of the waiters?'

'Oh, they're O.K. They won't say anything. It wouldn't do for them to.'

'I think I prefer not. But I can give you a whisky-and-soda.'

'Thanks, Carolus,' said the youth who believed he was in a situation he understood well.

Carolus rounded on him suddenly.

'A man stayed here on the night of Imogen Marvell's death. He had been here on a previous occasion and complained of food poisoning.' Carolus saw that Dave Paton was watching him with sullen but close attention. 'On that occasion you followed him out to his car and spoke to him. Why?'

'Here, what *is* this?' asked Paton defensively. 'You the law, or something?'

'Never mind what I am. Answer my question.'

'Why should I?'

'Because it's in your own interest. I'm investigating a number of things here.'

It was not much of a bluff but it seemed to work.

'Is that what you sent for me for?' Dave's tone was less resentful.

'For nothing else. Why did you follow that man to his car that night?'

'I heard he owned a restaurant, if you want to know.'

'Well?'

'I've had enough of this place.'

'I see. And did he?'

'No. They must have been pulling my leg.'

'Who must?'

'It was Tom who told me. Tom Bridger, that is. He said the man owned a restaurant and why didn't I try for a job? So I went out and asked him.'

'What did he say?'

'Turned nasty. Shouted. "No I *don't* own a restaurant and if I did own a restaurant I certainly shouldn't employ someone

86

working in a place where I'd been poisoned." I told him he hadn't been poisoned here. If there's one thing Tony's strict on it's cleanliness.'

'Tony?'

'Antoine, you call him. The *chef*. But this character wouldn't have it. He went on about poisoning till he drove off.'

'You had never seen him before?'

'Not so far as I know. Why? Did he do for Imogen Marvell?'

Ignoring this Carolus asked Dave if he was sure it was Bridger who had sent him across.

'Yeh. He was pulling my leg. There's a lot of that in the kitchen. Even old Tony who looks like a funeral doesn't mind a joke now'n again. Tom's always at it. But I want to get away.'

'Why?'

'There's things I don't like.'

'Such as?'

'Personal things.'

'Like Gloria Gee?'

'She was all right with me for a time till Tom stuck his nose in.'

'I see. Unrequited love.'

Dave used an explosive monosyllable in the plural. 'Anyway,' he added, 'she's gone on Rolland. God knows why. But his old woman found out about it.'

'About what?'

'Whatever there was between them. She came in here one day unexpected and found them in the cellar—checking bottles, *they* said. Since then Rolland doesn't dare look at Gloria. His wife's a proper old tartan.'

'Tartar,' corrected Carolus.

87

'Well, she is. It's her got the money, you see. Now Rolland's scared to speak to Gloria she takes it out on me.'

'And on Bridger?'

'Not so much on Tom. Anyhow, I want to go somewhere where I can get on. Learn a bit more.'

'You told Imogen Marvell you did enjoy the work.'

'That was for her, the silly cow,' said Dave impatiently. "Do you enjoy your work, my little man?" What's she know about food, anyway? I'd like to see her deal with thirty or forty lunches at a time, all ordered *à la carte*. That's what we do.'

'You think you could do it on your own?'

'In a small place, yes. Sure I could.'

'How do you think Imogen Marvell came to suffer from food poisoning? Because she undoubtedly did.'

'You know what I think? I think she took something specially to upset her.'

'With what motive?'

'Just to make trouble. She's that sort of woman. It couldn't have been the *scampi*. They're kept in the deep freeze and only got out when they're ordered.'

'Who got them out that day?'

'I did. And Tom made up the dish. If there had been one of them *off* I'd have seen it.'

'Antoine had nothing to do with it?'

'No. He was doing something else.'

'Who else handled that particular dish?'

'No one. Only Stefan in the dining-room, I suppose. Or whoever served it. It has to be *flambé* at the table.'

'Mrs Boot wasn't there that night?'

'No. She only comes on Thursdays when I'm off.'

'Tell me, Dave, did you go straight to bed when you'd

finished work? On the night Imogen Marvell died, I mean.'

'Me?'

Dave wanted a few seconds for reflection.

'Yes. You.'

'Not straight to bed, no. As a matter of fact I went to a dance. Over at Netterly.'

'How did you get there?'

'Friend of mine in the village. Has a car. Took us over for the last bit of the dance.'

'Us?'

'I went with Ali and Abdul. Anything wrong with that?'

'Nothing. What time did you leave the dance?'

' 'Bout one, it must have been.'

'And came straight back?'

'I don't see what that's to do with you, whatever you're investigating. As a matter of fact this friend of mine from the village and I had a couple of birds to take home.'

'Quite. What time did you get back?'

'Couldn't have been much before four o'clock.'

'And the two Moroccans?'

'Didn't see them again after the dance. We thought they'd got a lift back.'

'Had they?'

'I don't know. They don't say much. They turned up here in the morning, I know that.'

'And when you got back at whatever time it was did you see anyone about?'

'You're giving me a grilling, aren't you?'

'I'm incurably inquisitive.'

'As a matter of fact I did. I met Tony.'

'Antoine? But he lives in the village, doesn't he?'

89

'Yes. Wife and two children. But I saw him.'

'Did he see you?'

'No. My friend was dropping me down the road a few yards. I was just going to get out of his old barrow after we'd sat talking there for a bit . . .'

'With the lights of the car off?'

'Yes. But he switched them on for me to get out and I saw Tony coming towards us. I told my friend to switch off again and stayed there till he had passed. He must have been going home. He probably thought we were a couple having a go in the car. He didn't look into the car as he passed.'

'How do you get on with Antoine?'

'He's all right. Bit of an old sourpuss. He thinks he ought to own the place with Rolland. They were partners once and Tony's a good cook. Knows more than Rolland will ever know.'

'Were you surprised to see him coming away from the hotel at that time?'

'Not all that surprised. Now and again he has a game of poker with Stefan and Molt. That's if Stefan's not boozed up.'

'They both live in the men's quarters?'

'Yea. Molt's left his wife. She doesn't know where he is. Molt's not his real name.'

'How do you know?'

'You hear things in a pub like this. She's looking for him and he's scared because he owes god knows what maintenance. Stefan's wife's left *him,* and gone off with a Belgian. So they both live as bachelors.'

'You think all three were playing poker that night?'

'Not my business, but that's what I thought at the time.'

'And now?'

'I don't really think any different. Only it seems funny the old girl kicked it that night.'

'Hilariously funny.'

'You know what I mean. When I got indoors there wasn't a sound. I suppose they were all asleep. There was no light under any of the doors anyway. I dropped off at once.'

'There's one other thing . . .'

'Haven't you asked me enough?' said Dave with affected weariness.

'Have you seen anyone else talking to the man who complained about food poisoning? Either when he first came or when he returned on the night of Imogen Marvell's death?'

Dave looked at him with wide open eyes.

'No. I haven't. Did anyone talk to him?'

It sounded frank and convincing.

'Thanks for your information,' Carolus said.

'Thanks for the drink, Carolus,' Dave grinned. 'I hope you catch 'em.'

When he had gone Carolus sat for a time in the one armchair provided and thought deeply. The makings of an interesting but ugly possibility was beginning to form in his mind. After ten minutes he rang the bell.

Ali, one of the North Africans, appeared.

'Still on duty?' Carolus asked him.

'No. Finished,' he said smiling.

'Then you can sit down and talk to me. I want to ask you a few questions.'

Unlike the English whom he had interrogated Ali questioned neither his right nor his motive in asking questions but sat obediently in a chair and waited.

'You are Moroccan?'

91

'Yes. My brother is Algerian.'

'How?'

Ali shrugged. 'He is born in Algeria. His father and mother Algerian.

'But he is your brother?'

'We are brothers. We work together two years now.'

Metaphorically brothers, Carolus noted.

'You like working here?'

'Yes.' But it might just as well have been 'No' for all the information it gave.

'And Abdul?'

'He wants his wife here. From Algeria.'

Enough of preliminaries, Carolus thought.

'Ali, you were serving dinner on the night Miss Marvell was taken ill?'

'Yes.'

'Did you notice two men who sat at a table near hers?'

It was obvious that the short answer was 'Yes' but that was not Ali's way.

'One thin and tall?'

'Yes. Fairly thin.'

'One more heavy?'

'Yes.'

'I saw them. They had been here before.'

'A few days earlier?'

'Yes.'

'You did not speak to them?'

'To one, I did. I remembered him. I worked long time in London night club. The VIP. He came there.'

'What was he called?'

'I don't know a name. All called him Maxie.'

'Not Jimmie?'

'No. Maxie.'

'What did he say when you recognised him?'

'He don't say anything. He no remember me.'

'Did you see him alone when he was here?'

'Just a minute, I see him without the other one. I said, "Hullo, Mr Maxie". He say a bad word. "—— off", he say. So I don't speak any more to him.'

'What about the man who was taken ill at table?'

'Very noisy,' reflected Ali.

'Had you ever seen him before?'

'No.'

'Did he speak to you at all while he was here?'

'Only at the table. For a salad.'

'I see. Now you remember the night Miss Marvell died?'

'I don't remember nothing. I don't see nothing.'

'Where did you go when you finished work that night?'

'I go sleep.'

The lie was not necessarily ill-intentioned. It was a matter of instinctively taking cover.

'At once? When you finished work?'

'I sleep.'

'Abdul too?'

'He sleep. He sleep more than me.'

'You didn't go out in a car?'

'What you talking about? What car you mean?'

'With Dave Paton and his friend? To a dance at Netterly?'

Ali's recovery was magnificent.

'Why *not* I go to a dance? Work all finished.'

'No reason at all. I just asked.'

'Certainly I go to a dance. Abdul too. I like dancing. I dance very good.'

'When did it finish?'

'I don't know. My watch broken.'

'Did you leave with Abdul?'

Ali had become cautious.

'Leave where?'

'The dance.'

'Yes. With Abdul.'

'Then what did you do?'

'There was no car,' said Ali, playing for time.

'So?'

'So we started walking home. We were walking all night. It was bloody damn cold.'

'What time did you get back?'

'In time for work.'

'It took you a long time. Netterly's only four miles away.'

'We lose our way. We are in the dark. No light. No people. In the country, in the night. We walk and walk. Abdul say one way, I say another way. We bloody damn walked all night till we found the way home.'

It could be true, Carolus reflected. He gave Ali a pound note and dismissed him. For the first time he locked his bedroom door that night.

Ten

It appeared that the solicitor who had drawn Imogen's will was expected back from a continental holiday and the incongruous people who had been about her at her death had decided to remain at the Fleur-de-Lys until they had learned the contents of that important document.

Carolus had observed them at meals and thought what a very odd trio they made, Dudley Smithers as unruffled as before, Miss Trudge weepy and vague, and Grace Marvell severely matter-of-fact and curt with both of them.

Meanwhile he wanted an interview, which he foresaw as difficult, with the assistant *chef*, Tom Bridger. This jolly character, all smiles and good nature to outward appearance, certainly had information which would clear at least a bit of the problem but it would be very difficult to make him part with it. On the whole he believed that a mixture of menace and bluff, with a certain amount of *bonhomie*, the technique so often used with success by the police, might be most effective.

He arranged the *mise en scène* with some care, borrowing Rolland's office for the purpose and sending for Bridger at ten o'clock in the morning as though he had some super-policial authority. He invited him to sit down, offered him a cigarette, met his good-humoured smile with a stiff one of his own, then opened broadside.

95

'You know some offices with a flat above them on the first and second floors of Gaitskell Mansions, Attlee Avenue, Bayswater,' Carolus stated rather than enquired.

He watched Bridger's face and saw the smile disappear as though it had been switched off at the main. But Bridger remained silent.

'The offices are in the name of Montreith,' added Carolus, as though to assist Bridger's memory.

Still an uncomfortable, not to say tense, silence.

'Why, I wonder, did you try to make it appear that Dave Paton was the local representative by sending him out to speak to the man who had complained of food poisoning. You told Paton he was a restaurant proprietor. Remember?'

Still no verbal reaction but Bridger was not a good actor.

'It would have been far wiser to try to implicate Ali who had known the so-called Rivers as Maxie at a night club called the VIP. That might have worked.'

'I don't know what you're talking about,' said Bridger at last.

'Then there was your interesting conversation with this same man, who calls himself Mandeville. You must remember that. In the Spinning Wheel Café. You went there by appointment.'

'I don't know what on earth you're talking about,' repeated Bridger.

'No? Then I'll tell you. I'm talking about murder. Extortion, violence, blackmail as well, but more particularly murder, in which you are involved. Enough altogether to send you down for thirty years. What about a drink?'

Bridger nodded.

'It's best to come to the point, I always think,' said Carolus when he had ordered by telephone two large whiskies. 'We can waste so much time going round it.'

'Who are you?' asked Bridger.

'Just a very inquisitive individual who is not very impressed with a firm trying to work the American protection racket in England. The island's too small and the penalties too great. Tell me, Bridger, did you get into this of your own accord or are you a victim too?'

'I don't know what . . .'

'Now don't say that again because it simply isn't true. You know exactly what I'm talking about. What you didn't know until now is that you're for it. In a big way. The train robber sentences will be nothing to what your crowd's going to get.'

'I'm not saying anything.'

'No? Up to you, of course. You've told me all I really want to know.'

'I haven't said a word!' For the first time Bridger showed real and immediate alarm. A nebulous thirty years' sentence was nothing, it seemed, to the dangers of having spoken.

'You'll have to convince your friends of that. They will wonder, inevitably, how I know all I do—about you and about them.'

Bridger looked up with relief when Abdul brought the drinks Carolus had ordered and swallowed his greedily.

'I'm afraid you're between the devil and the deep blue sea. But the devil can't win this time and the deep blue sea is wide and full of possibilities for the future. The future may be remote in your case, but there is a future.'

Suddenly Bridger looked at Carolus keenly and said, 'Can I trust you?'

'Oh no,' said Carolus. 'If you mean to keep you out of this

thing, not for a moment. When I've got all my facts straight I'm going to make a report. I happen to dislike blackmail almost as much as murder. You can only trust me not to let your friends know where I got the information you're about to give me. On that you can have my word.'

'What information?' asked Bridger desperately.

'Bits and pieces here and there. To fill in the gaps.'

'I don't know much.'

'I don't suppose you do. Not enough to get you off if you give Queen's Evidence. But enough to save your life, probably. That wouldn't be worth much if your friends thought you had been chatting me up, would it?'

The question was rhetorical. Bridger knew that it did not need an answer.

'I'm afraid this is your only chance to decide. Things like this can't be left in the air. You can talk to me now. I shan't be available again. The mills will start grinding after this.'

'If I tell you what you want to know, will you do what you can for me when . . .'

'When the whole thing blows up? I make no promise at all. It depends on how much you are involved. There has been at least one murder here.'

'I haven't had a penny out of it.'

'You will, Bridger. You will. Unless things develop more quickly than I imagine.'

'What do you want to know?'

'First of all, how you got into this.'

Bridger swallowed.

'I was minding my own business. Doing my job. Then all of a sudden I got a phone call. About three weeks ago. Someone asked me if I'd be free to take over the kitchens of a new restaurant being opened. I was to be *chef* at nearly twice what I'm earning now. The man telephoning me said I was to meet him at the Red Horse at Netterly on my evening off. So I went and found it was Rivers and Razor Gray.'

Carolus nodded. This was the sort of thing he expected.

'Nothing more was said about the restaurant,' went on Bridger. 'They asked me if I would join in a little joke they were playing on Rolland.'

'A *joke*?'

'Yes. That's what they said. When Imogen Marvell came down on her annual visit. All I had to do was put a few drops of something in her food. Fish, it worked best with. It was just a simple emetic, they said.'

'What were they to pay you for that?'

'A hundred nicker.'

'Rather an expensive joke.'

'That's what I thought.'

'But you agreed?'

'Not straight away. They said let's go to another pub. Rivers was laughing. It seemed all right and I got in the car. Before I knew where I was we were going into those Gaitskell Mansions you mentioned. I noticed the name but I didn't know till you told me where they were.'

Once started Bridger seemed glad to get the story off his chest.

'There seemed to be a lot of them there. Ugly-looking crowd. They introduced me to one man sitting at a desk. I suppose he was the boss.'

'Montreith?'

'That's what they called him.'

'What did he look like?'

'Pale, pasty-looking. About forty-five. Cold, nasty eyes. Rivers was laughing. "He doesn't know whether he wants to join in our little joke," he said. Montreith didn't laugh. He just looked at me and said, "Show him our friend in the next room." They did. There was a fellow lying on the floor stripped off. He'd had the worst beating-up I've ever seen. Eyes closed right up. He was holding his stomach and groaning but only half-conscious, I thought. Terrible sight.'

'So you agreed?'

'What else could I do? But I tell you what I did when I got back here. I tried a couple of drops of the stuff on myself. I wasn't going to poison anyone right out. All it did was to make me sick as a dog.'

'Have another drink?' suggested Carolus.

With the first faint smile he had given since Carolus had begun questioning, Bridger said he thought he would.

'I soon realised what they were after. Protection money from Rolland. Rivers told me in the end when he'd made sure I was with them. They work it on big restaurants and clubs and places. Several of them go and raise hell one way or another if they're not paid off. But with famous restaurants they work this food poisoning lark. At least they're prepared to. Most of them pay up.'

'How do you know?'

'Rivers told me.'

'Any names?'

'Yes. He mentioned the Old Cygnet Inn.'

'Good gracious.'

The Old Cygnet attempted to emulate the Cheddar Cheese, or Simpson's, or Scott's, serving very English food mostly to American visitors to London.

'And the Tourterelle.'

'They're certainly enterprising. You mean to say those pay?'

'What else can they do? Montreith must be making enormous money. He's clever. It's wonderful cover, being a solicitor. All sorts going to his office. He's known for arranging the defence of criminals. The thing's on a big scale. Once I was in with them there was no getting out. I had to do what they said.'

'What do you know about Mandeville?'

'I should say he's kept for the kind of job he did here. Probably he's straight, on the outside. Got a correct address and that.'

'Did you fix his food?'

'No. There was no need. He did it himself.'

'But Imogen Marvell?'

'Yes. In the *scampi*.'

'It was indirectly the cause of her death.'

'I wasn't to know that. I gave her an emetic, that's all.'

'And you've been told to do nothing more?'

'Not yet, but I shall be, for certain. They'll close this place if Rolland doesn't pay. Then they'll get me a job somewhere else. There's no getting away.'

'Unless they're broken.'

'I don't know how you're going to do it. It's a powerful organisation.'

'I think something can be managed,' said Carolus quietly. 'But there are one or two more questions I should like to ask you.'

'Well. I've gone so far. You may as well know the lot,' said Bridger, a suggestion of his customary good humour returning.

'For instance, about those premises in Gaitskell Mansions.

Could they have been a normal solicitor's offices?'

'Not when I saw them late at night. Not with that crowd standing about. But in the daytime I suppose they could.'

'And the other room you went into?'

'It's a funny thing but as I remember it there was no window. Of course I was chiefly noticing the poor chap on the floor. But that's the impression I got.'

'Could be,' said Carolus. 'It probably had a sound-proof door as well.'

Bridger made a sound usually interpreted as 'Urgh!'

'You didn't see the interior staircase which is supposed to lead to the flat above?'

'No. I didn't know about that.'

'Something else. Do you think anyone else here, on the hotel staff or otherwise, is involved in this?'

Bridger answered quickly. To quickly, Carolus thought.

'I wouldn't know, would I? I'd be the last person they'd tell. Unless you mean Rolland.'

'You're quite friendly with Antoine?'

'Tony? Yes. He's all right.'

'And Stefan?'

'Don't see much of him.'

'What about Molt?'

'Don't know much about him.'

'Do you ever play poker with them?'

'I have done. I'm not keen on cards.'

'You've no reason to think any of them suspects you of . . . collaboration?'

'No. I suppose Stefan might. He's a clever man. Only drink's his trouble.'

'So I understand.'

'And you don't think Rolland knows anything about you?'
Bridger considered.

'I'm pretty sure he doesn't. He must think someone here is in the lark. Otherwise how could Marvell have been given anything to upset her. He's more likely to suspect Tony.'

'Perhaps,' said Carolus drily.

'I've got to get to work,' said Bridger.

Carolus's manner changed abruptly.

'Wait a minute. I haven't asked you the most important questions of all.'

Bridger sat up. There was a new atmosphere in the room. Bridger seemed suddenly watchful.

'You were on the first-floor landing on the night Imogen Marvell died.' He let that sink in, then added: 'I saw you myself.'

There was silence then Bridger tried to grin.

'What about it?'

'I'm asking you.'

'I don't see what that's got to do with you. If you know so much you should know where I was going.'

'I know where you're going to *say* you were going. To Gloria Gee's room.'

'So what?'

'Oh nothing. If you *were* going to Gloria's room. Or rather coming away from it when I saw you.'

'Where do you think I had been?'

'I'm very anxious to know, Bridger.'

'Why don't you ask Gloria?'

'That's a foolish question. You knew Mandeville was in the hotel that night?'

'Yes. But I didn't know which room.'

'You could see that from the register.'

'I wasn't interested. What are you trying to make out? You think I had anything to do with Imogen Marvell's death?'

He had become red and indignant.

'All I've said so far is that you were indirectly responsible. Did you see Mandeville at Gaitskell Mansions?'

'No.'

It was almost shouted.

'What was he here for that night?'

'I don't know. I've told you all I know. It's no good asking me about Mandeville.'

'I'm asking you about yourself. You've told me how you came to be in this thing. But you haven't told me everything. I'd like to know a great deal more about your movements on the night Imogen Marvell died.'

Bridger was distressed—and frightened.

'I went to see Gloria. Then I went to bed.'

'At what time?'

'About half past one.'

'Was anyone about?'

'There was a light under Stefan's door. That's all.'

'You saw no one on your way back to your quarters?'

'No one at all. And that's all I've got to say.'

As though waiting to see whether Carolus would say any more he rose slowly.

'Listen to me,' said Carolus. 'I don't know how far you are in this. You certainly helped Montreith to blackmail Rolland. In other words from the gang's point of view you know too much. I oughtn't to give you this advice, but why don't you disappear for a time?'

Bridger looked sulky.

'I can't. I haven't the money. They haven't paid me yet.'

'I warn you, I think you're in danger. I shan't tell anyone what you have told me but Montreith may gather from what I do that I know too much. He may guess my information comes from you. That would mean danger—to say the least of it. So I'm warning you.'

'I can't go away now,' said Bridger, and made for the door.

Eleven

Carolus went straight from the office to Gloria's bar. She gave him a sly smile.

'I didn't know you were a detective,' she said.

'But I'm not.'

'Well, sort of. I'm glad you're not like James Bond, though. I'm tired of him. I say, have you heard what's happened? Imogen Marvell's solicitor has come. He's with the three of them now. In the Residents' Lounge. I'd love to know what's going on. Wouldn't you?'

They had not to wait long. A red-eyed Miss Trudge hurried in and took a straight-up armchair as though she was in desperate need of support. Carolus offered her a drink and this time there was no coy hesitation.

'I will!' she said. 'Thank you. Brandy, please. I think perhaps I need a double.'

'Is something wrong?'

'Yes . . . oh, everything really.' She became somewhat incoherent. 'It's cruel . . . after all those years . . . I can't believe . . . there must be some mistake . . . She couldn't have . . .'

'You've had bad news?'

'Imogen's will . . . the solicitor came down from London . . . he was very kind about it . . . It's wicked, really . . . I've been cut out . . . after years of . . .'

She dissolved. The double brandy she had finished was not, Carolus perceived, the first she had drunk that morning.

'I could never have believed . . . so deceitful . . . and her poor sister . . . Everything to her husband . . . Everything. Even that little emerald brooch she promised me . . . How could she?'

Grace stormed in.

'Don't sit there blubbering, Maud,' she said sharply. 'We must *do* something. We're going to fight this tooth and nail. How *dare* she do this? We'll dispute the whole thing.'

Miss Trudge showed unexpected shrewdness.

'On what grounds?' she asked. Then, succumbing again to tears, 'I can't believe it. That little emerald . . . it's so cruel. They hadn't spoken for years . . .'

'It's an act of spite,' said Grace. 'Nothing else. I taught her all she knew. A kind act never goes unpunished.'

Miss Trudge managed to lay a ten-shilling note on the counter.

'Just a teeny . . . double,' she said. 'I feel I need . . . Not even the furniture . . .'

'Oh, shut up, Maud. This is just as she intended you to behave. Pull yourself together, woman. We've got to fight. I shall sue the estate for . . .'

Mr Smithers entered.

'Good morning,' he said politely to Gloria. 'A grapefruit juice, please.'

He opened his newspaper, and taking his drink went calmly to a table. Miss Trudge watched him, then with a strangled cry of indignation swallowed her drink, burst into tears and ran from the room.

'You realise, don't you,' said Grace to Smithers, 'that I shall fight this all along the line. You're not going to get away with it.'

Smithers looked up.

'What? Oh, that,' he said and returned to his paper.

'Yes *that*,' said Grace, growing in her turn somewhat hysterical. 'It's monstrous, and you know it. But if you think for a single moment that I'm going to stand by and let you grab ...'

'I should have thought this was hardly the place to discuss family matters,' said Smithers primly. He sipped his grapefruit juice.

'But what are you going to *do*?' cried Grace.

'I shall be returning to town on the 2.47.'

Grace received this announcement with a snort and left the room.

Mr Smithers put down his newspaper and addressed Carolus.

'A little brighter this morning,' he observed.

'Much,' said Carolus sitting down unbidden beside him.

'I shall be sorry to return to London. It has been most pleasant down here.'

'Rather disturbing for you, surely?'

Mr Smithers smiled.

'Oh, I take things very much as they come, you know. We all have ups and downs.'

'Very philosophical of you.' Then determined to break this complacency Carolus asked: 'Do you think your wife was murdered?'

Mr Smithers seemed undisturbed by the question.

'It's a moot point, isn't it?' he said chattily.

'Were you satisfied with the coroner's verdict?'

'Oh, I *think* so. There appears to be no doubt that she died of suffocation. I believe such cases are not infrequent. I remember reading of one quite recently. In Plymouth, I seem to recall. Or was it Portsmouth? I don't know the South Coast very well, I'm afraid, though I'm told it's very attractive. I usually take my holidays in Wales.'

'Your wife seemed somewhat excitable,' said Carolus, trying to draw Mr Smithers back from topography.

'Somewhat, perhaps. No, it was Penzance. I remember now. A young child. Funny I should not have recalled it at once. I have an excellent memory.'

'I understand you are the sole beneficiary under your wife's will.'

'Yes. That is so. Quite a considerable estate, I believe. The career she made for herself was most lucrative. I was never much interested in gastronomy myself. Now if it had been gasteropods it would have been another matter. I have studied the snail—a most interesting mollusc.'

'Reputed to move slowly but to get there in the end.'

'Exactly.'

'Leaving a trail behind it.'

'Like so many of us!' agreed Mr Smithers.

'If I were a newspaperman I should ask you some impertinent questions about your unexpected windfall.'

'Oh, it wasn't unexpected. Not at all. And I never think questions are impertinent. They show one's interest.'

'Then I will ask you, how did you feel about this very large fortune?'

'Most gratified,' said Mr Smithers.

'Will it change your manner of life much?'

'Oh, not in the least. Why should it? I dislike change.'

'Are you going to endow a favourite charity?'

'I have none, really. I find that the advertisements of most charitable causes are crude attempts to invade one's privacy. Such very insistent appeals. No, I see no reason to encourage that sort of thing.'

'And Miss Trudge?' ventured Carolus.

'I shall feel bound to respect my late wife's wishes. Had it been her intention that Miss Trudge should benefit she would have made arrangements to that end.'

'Very logical.'

'I have always been considered a logical man. Life would be chaotic without logic, wouldn't it? And it's chaotic enough already.'

'Did you see your wife on the evening of her death?' asked Carolus abruptly. Surely that would crack the shell?

'Oh, I expect so. I must surely have looked in before I went to bed.'

'Do you remember the time?'

'Of course. Ten forty-five. My invariable bedtime.'

'And you looked in on your wife?'

'I would scarcely say "looked". Miss Trudge had warned me that she was sleeping off an injection. I did not put the light on.'

'Or speak?'

'I expect I just whispered something. But there was no reply.'

'You heard her breathing, no doubt. Under drugs people breathe rather stertorously, usually.'

'My hearing is not quick. I don't remember hearing any sound at all.'

'So, Mr Smithers, it is possible that your wife was already dead when you went to her room?'

'Quite possible,' agreed Mr Smithers cheerfully.

'In which case she must have died before ten forty-five?'

'Say ten-fifty.'

'Miss Trudge was with her till ten-twenty.'

'In that case, if Imogen was dead when I looked in she must have died between ten-twenty and ten-fifty, mustn't she? The coroner would like to have known that.'

'But we aren't sure that she was dead when you went to her room.'

'Indeed no. We are not sure of anything. We can only hazard a guess. It reminds me of a recent case in the papers . . .'

'At Penzance?' suggested Carolus bitterly.

'No. This was at Cardiff. Or was it Carlisle? An elderly man and his wife found gassed in a bedroom. It was impossible to know which was responsible. Carmarthen, that was it. I was most interested because I frequently pass through there when I'm on holiday.'

'You did not look into your wife's room again that night?'

'I am fortunate in being an extremely good sleeper. I go to bed as I have explained at ten forty-five. By eleven-fifteen I am fast asleep and rarely wake before eight a.m. Something altogether exceptional would have to take place to awaken me.'

'Something altogether exceptional *did* take place. Your wife died.'

Mr Smithers brushed this aside.

'Oh yes,' he said airily. 'But we were unaware of that, were we not, until the secretary caused all that hubbub in the morning. It disturbed me at a very early hour.'

'You were unable to sleep again?' asked Carolus with what was intended as bitter irony.

'Oh quite,' said Mr Smithers. 'Once awakened I remain

awake. It is a law of nature for me. I dressed and came down-stairs only to find that no breakfast was served before eight o'clock. A most discouraging start to the day. Later as you know I saw the doctor and completed all the necessary for-malities.'

'That must have been trying for you.'

'It was. Most distasteful. I am quite unused to dealing with situations of this kind.'

'There aren't many fortunately. You said a few minutes ago that the contents of Imogen Marvell's will were not unexpected by you. Had she herself informed you of them?'

The conversation had taken on more and more the form of an interrogation with no holds barred; but Mr Smithers seemed not in the least put out. In fact he appeared rather to enjoy it.

'Yes, indeed. About three months ago she wrote to me ask-ing me to call. I dislike the telephone and have always refused to instal it. I find it disturbs one's curriculum.'

'And you called?'

'I did. The secretary, Miss Trudge, was absent that day. I was alone with my wife. We had seen little of one another for some ten years. I found her manner of life repugnant to me. She seemed to *seek* disturbance and publicity. We had long ago realised our incompatability and surrendered to it.'

'But she wanted to see you?'

'Yes. She told me her difficulties. She was, it seemed, sur-rounded by disloyal and unappreciative natures. Her sister she stigmatised as commonplace and unable to understand her more subtle temperament. Her secretary failed to perceive Imogen's extraordinary qualities. Both thought only of them-selves and were eager to possess themselves of Imogen's estate after her death which, she felt, might not long be delayed. I protested at that and she said, "Whom the Gods love die young", and added that I should never know what mean and malicious jealousy surrounded her.

'Then she told me. It wasn't that she wished to benefit me, she said, but she was determined that none of her entourage or employees should receive anything on her death and by leaving her money to me she could ensure this. If she left it to some charity or other they might find a means of disputing it. But since it would be left to her husband no one could do so. I acquiesced.'

'You bet you did,' thought Carolus vulgarly.

'The matter would be carried out immediately. She gave me the name of the solicitors who were drawing up her will and bound me to secrecy on the whole matter. I respected my promise not to reveal her intentions and neither her sister nor Miss Trudge had any notion that her previous will, leaving them substantially provided for, had been superseded. Until this morning. They seemed to be quite upset,' ended Mr Smithers gently.

'They were,' said Carolus.

'That shows the folly of counting one's chickens in the matter of wills and bequests. We must all have known examples of that. There was a case in Northampton . . .'

'And you feel no sympathy for these two?'

'Feeling sympathy with misfortune is not a habit I cultivate. I am a simple individual who asks nothing of the world but to be left to my own modest devices. If I were to express any sympathy it would be with Mrs de Mornay who was my wife's housekeeper in Rutland Gate. A most deserving woman.'

Mr Smithers glanced at an old-fashioned watch which he drew from his waistcoat pocket.

'It appears to be time for lunch,' he said and with an equable smile left Carolus to ponder over his astonishing confidences.

Stefan was cool and sober at lunch and Carolus took the opportunity of speaking to him.

'I should like very much to have a few words with you,' he said. 'I am investigating certain matters here. Could that be managed?'

'Certainly. When?' said Stefan indicating something on the menu as though they were innocently discussing this.

'This afternoon?'

'I shall be free by three o'clock.'

'Come out to the car park at the back. We'll drive out somewhere.'

Stefan nodded, and appeared to write down Carolus's order.

He was a very different man away from his work.

'There's a country club beyond Netterly where we can get a drink in the afternoon,' he said, and Carolus drove away not knowing whether they had been observed or not.

Stefan proved to be both intelligent and cultured. He readily admitted that he gathered there was some kind of blackmail or protection racket going on but said he had not been approached by anyone. Rolland had warned him to be on his guard in the restaurant against anyone who seemed to want to cause trouble but had not told him anything in advance against Mandeville.

'He's obviously very scared and I don't blame him,' said Stefan. 'I've heard of this sort of thing before. It's difficult to cope with because people are afraid to give evidence. Do you connect it with the Marvell's death?'

This was a question which Carolus himself would like to have put and he evaded it by saying: 'Do you?'

'I thought the coroner was too easily satisfied,' Stefan said. 'I was not asked anything except about the scene in the dining-room.'

'Had you anything to say?'

'I don't know whether it's relevant or not but there was a small incident.'

'Really?'

'During her last afternoon the Marvell asked for me personally and I went up to her room. She was perfectly calm so I can't help thinking that her hysterics afterwards were a bit forced. She said she wanted a bottle of champagne put on the ice and brought up to her at half past nine. No one was to know about it and I was to bring it myself. "Just as a night-cap," she said.'

'You took it up?'

'Of course. I didn't know she'd been given an injection to make her sleep. I went up at just half past nine with a bottle of Veuve Clicquot. I knocked at the door but there was no answer. So I went in.'

'The light was on?'

'No. And I did not switch it on—there was enough light from the passage. She was snoring like a pig. I put the tray down on a table near her bed. Not on the bedside table—there wasn't room. Then I tiptoed out.'

'You are sure there was no one else in the room?'

'Pretty sure. But the door into the bathroom was shut.'

'What happened to the bottle?'

'One of the Moroccan boys brought it down in the morning. It was empty. I hope the poor secretary had it. It was good champagne.'

Twelve

This was not bringing Carolus any nearer to information about Montreith and he decided to visit the Old Cygnet Inn. This meant that long and tedious approach to London which drivers from the provinces know and Carolus reflected that any one of the 150 horses whose power was theoretically concentrated in his engine could have drawn him for the last ten miles in a third of the time before the coming of motor cars.

However by putting his car in an underground car park a mile away and securing a taxi he eventually reached the Old Cygnet at shortly after eleven. George Porter, the much photographed proprietor, had just reached his office.

The Old Cygnet had been constructed from antique materials on a site once occupied by an inn of that name. It was dark with oak blackened, some of it, by time and smoke, some by artificial means. The architecture was so Tudor that one's head was in constant danger of being bumped by overhanging beams and its decoration included a miscellany of eighteenth century curios, warming-pans, horse-brasses, hunting horns, all the familiar items from the shops of the more conventional antique dealers. It was served by 'wenches' in mob caps and waiters wearing leather aprons and knee-breeches.

Mr Porter resembled, and intended to resemble, the caricaturist's image of John Bull, complete with side-whiskers. He at first refused to see Carolus who had sent in his name as John Barber but on being told that Carolus was a friend of Mr Rivers had him admitted to his office.

'Well?' he said.

Carolus affected to be no less terse.

'We're bringing out a guide-book of restaurants and clubs,' said Carolus.

'Who is we?'

'You know who we are. Advertisement space costs a hundred quid an inch. I've put you down for two inches.'

Mr Porter flushed furiously.

'I don't want it.'

Carolus started to rise.

'Very well. I'll tell them,' he said.

'This is monstrous,' said Mr Porter.

'Think so?'

'I never undertook . . .'

'No. This is something new. A pet scheme of the boss's. He's very keen on it. Very keen. He expects to get full collaboration.'

'Not from me,' said Mr Porter. 'I've done enough already.'

'You know your own business best.'

'I told Rivers distinctly that I would do no more.'

'This was unforeseen then.'

There was an impasse.

'How often is this supposed to appear?'

'It's an annual,' said Carolus. 'We did think of making it quarterly. Perhaps you'd like Rivers to come and see you about it?'

Mr Porter glared at him with open hostility.

'How do I know that something else like this won't crop up?'

'You don't. We're an enterprising firm. Always thinking out something new for our clients.'

'Blackguardly. I shan't pay. You can do what you like.'

'Unfortunate, that Imogen Marvell business,' said Carolus chattily.

Mr Porter stared.

'That?' he said. 'My God!'

'I'll be running along,' said Carolus.

'Wait a minute. Suppose I take an inch?'

'The boss won't be pleased,' said Carolus.

'The boss! Who is this boss you keep talking about? I don't believe he exists!'

'Perhaps you'd like to make his acquaintance? He might lunch here one day with some friends.'

'I'll take one inch. That must satisfy you.'

'In one pound notes, please,' said Carolus.

'I haven't got them. I can give you a cash cheque.'

Carolus smiled, he hoped grimly.

'Quite a sense of humour,' he said. 'Single pounds. I'll wait.'

After a moment Mr Porter left the room. He was gone for about four minutes and returned with a packet of treasury notes.

'You haven't been telephoning, or anything silly like that, I hope.'

'No. But it's the last time.'

He handed the packet across and Carolus threw it back.

'Mr Porter,' he said seriously. 'I have been satisfying myself that you are being blackmailed by a gang running a protection racket specialising in clubs and restaurants. I already know a good deal about these people and I mean to know more.'

Porter accepted this quickly.

'You the police?' he asked.

'No. A private individual.'

'What do you mean by coming to my office with this tale of a guide-book?'

'You lay yourself open to it. Haven't you the courage to expose this thing?'

'What thing? I know of no such thing. Rivers is a friend of mine.'

'*And* Razor Gray?'

'It's not the slightest use your coming to me for help. I shall simply deny this conversation.'

'But if the gang were broken?'

'How?'

'Arrested.'

'On other charges, you mean?'

'On sufficient charges to keep them indoors for twenty years. Would you have the courage *then* to help convict them?'

There was a pause.

'That's all in the air,' said Porter. 'I don't know who you are or what you're up to but you'll get nothing out of me. I'm not putting *my* head in a noose.'

'Do you know Gaitskell Mansions in Bayswater?'

'Never heard of them.'

'Ever met a man who calls himself Mandeville?'

'Don't know the name.'

'How much have you paid out already?'

'I haven't the slightest idea what you're talking about.'

'You're a coward, Porter. You want to see this ring broken to save your money but you won't lift a finger to help. Well, you may find you have to.'

'Will you kindly leave my office?'

Carolus walked out. In the restaurant as he passed through there was a heavy smell of roast meat. Baron of beef or haunch of venison? he wondered.

The Tourterelle when he found it had a very different *ambience,* being so extravagantly Gallic that a Frenchman would have recoiled. It looked expensive with its pseudo-*bistro* throw-away simplicity and the hand-written *à la carte* menu showing at the door proved that it was so. *Scampi à la Tourterelle* cost 30s., Carolus noted, and other items were proportionately priced. The *bistro* atmosphere was maintained inside where the waiters were casually dressed and the proprietor, whom Carolus recognised from published photographs, wore clothes that might have been designed by a Parisian *couturier.*

He approached Carolus.

' 'Ave you raysairved a table, m'sieur?' he asked.

'No. I'm afraid not.'

'All the tables are raysairved.'

'I'm a friend of Jimmie Rivers.'

There was a pause. Gaston Leroy was sizing Carolus up.

'This way, pliss,' he said shortly.

He was probably in his fifties, but with a cleverly designed blond wig and a face-lift he could have passed at a distance for thirty-seven. He minced rather than walked and took Carolus to a table in a corner. It was not yet one o'clock and the restaurant was still half empty.

He brought out a menu covering a large area of expensive paper and put it before Carolus at the same time whispering fiercely in his ear: 'If you start one thing, one single thing, I'm going to have you taken down the cellars and beaten up so

that your mother won't know you. Get that.' Then loudly:
'*M'sieur will have hors d'œuvres pair'aps?*'

'Half a dozen Whitstable oysters. Who said I was going to
cause trouble? Just came to see how you were getting on.'

'I'm getting on all right. No thanks to your lot. What do you
mean by sending that woman in here last week? *And to follow,
M'sieur?*'

'What woman?'

'*I 'ave some vairy good fæysan.* You know very well. She said
she'd found a cockroach in her food—the wicked bitch. The
waiter saw her getting it out of her bag.'

'*I think perhaps an entrecôte.* Things were in arrears,
weren't they? It's always best to keep up to date, then there
are no misunderstandings.'

'*The braised celairree?* You're a lot of wicked greedy
bastards, that's what you are, and you're not going to get away
with it much longer. I've got some here as tough as you are if
you start coming round again.'

'*Yes, that would be very nice.* Listen, Leroy. Take this in
quickly. I'm trying to smash that lot—I'm not one of them.
I want your help.'

'*Then to drink, sair?* What d'you mean? Are you the law?'
Carolus examined the wine card.

'No, I'm not the law. I'm a private individual. But I believe
I've got this lot. Do you know Montreith?'

'*Montrachet? Cairtainly, sair.* I'll talk to you later.'

Leroy approached a group which had just entered. To see
him leading two women and a man across the room one would
never have supposed he was a cockney who had built up a
reputation for French cooking and was now being blackmailed.
He looked sprightly and debonair.

The restaurant was now filled with prosperous-looking people. A very good business, Carolus thought, but scarcely able to meet the demands of Mr Montreith and his friends if these were the same as those made to Rolland.

Leroy approached again.

'*M'sieur's oysters were satisfactory?* Do you know Montreith by sight?'

Carolus shook his head.

'He has just come in with a woman. The third table from the door.'

'Does that mean trouble?'

'No. But expense, the wicked bloodsucker. Lunch, Champagne, everything of the best. It is intolerable.'

He moved away again walking with a peculiar springy motion and small steps.

Carolus looked across casually to the table indicated and saw a man who answered to Bridger's description, 'pale, pasty-looking, about forty-five, cold nasty eyes.' Yes, this could be Montreith. The eyes were curiously hooded. A killer, if ever there was one. A man of strong will-power, cruel and vain. The girl with him was well-dressed and did not look very intelligent.

Towards the end of the meal Leroy returned and whispered quickly: 'We could meet in the station buffet at four o'clock.'

'Good,' Carolus replied and added that he *would* have a brandy.

Leroy looked conspicuous in the unbeautiful surroundings of a station refreshment room but when Carolus had brought from the counter a cup of tea and taken the place beside him, the two men were free to talk without professional interpolations.

'*You* tell *me*, first,' said Leroy. 'What *is* your connection with this?'

'I do a certain amount of investigation in an amateur way. Chiefly murder. But a man who keeps a hotel and restaurant in the country came to me for help. He was being blackmailed under threats of disturbances and faked food poisoning in his restaurants, not to mention personal violence to himself.'

'That's Rolland,' decided Leroy.

'So I became interested. I discovered Montreith's place of business and flat.'

'How?'

'It doesn't matter. I know where it is. And I know at least three of you who are paying ransom.'

'Who's the third?'

'Porter of the Old Cygnet.'

Leroy seemed pleased at this.

'Is he really? Well! He can afford to. He gets the tourists with his steak-and-kidney pudding.'

'He's scared,' observed Carolus.

'Aren't we all? You don't know what it is to be in my position. I daren't go to the police. And what could the police do? There's no proof of anything.'

'I know it's difficult. But if once the police have enough evidence to arrest Montreith it would be different.'

'Suppose he got off? Where should I be then?'

'I think if you have followed recent cases you would find that the police don't move till they are sure of a conviction. And that means a good many years' sentence.'

'I daresay. But how can I chance it? I don't want to be dragged out of the river. Or lose my business.'

'I'll make a pact with you, Leroy. I won't ask you to make

a statement unless I'm quite satisfied that there will be no unpleasant consequences.'

'I don't know what to say. I feel I can trust you, though I don't know why I should. I know nothing about you.'

'True. But you've got to trust someone. You can't go *on* paying out blood money.'

'You mean you won't ask for a statement till Montreith is under arrest?'

'On very serious charges. Murder, perhaps. Certainly enough to put him away for years.'

'He might get bail.'

'No. There would be no bail in this case.'

'I'm not a man to be easily scared,' said Leroy, 'but these people are dangerous.'

'I know.'

'I suppose I'll have to agree. You may not believe it but it's that man coming in and ordering what he likes and never even asking for a bill which infuriates me far more than the actual money.'

'Yes. I think I can understand that.'

'All right then. When you tell me I can talk I will. But meanwhile you'll keep me out of it?'

'I will.'

'You think you can do this? Break them, I mean.'

'I think so.'

'I hope you do. It's a damnable thing. What will you get out of it?'

'Oh, a certain personal satisfaction. "Something attempted, something done, has earned a night's repose." And there are other questions to which I am looking for an answer. I want to know how Imogen Marvell died.'

'You don't think they . . . ?'

'I don't think anything at all, at least not aloud. You had better leave here first, Leroy.'

'All right. I suppose I shall hear from you?'

'Or *of* me, yes.'

'Good luck to you then.'

He stood up and Carolus watched him go out with his springy steps. He continued to sit there for ten minutes before leaving the buffet. Then he waited at the station entrance for a taxi and told the driver to take him to the car park where he had left the Bentley Continental. From there he drove to Rutland Gate.

Thirteen

The door of the late Imogen Marvell's house was opened by her housekeeper who had been described by Mr Smithers as 'a most deserving woman'. Deserving of what? Carolus wondered when he saw her.

Though nowadays the London districts can no longer be said to produce types, Mrs de Mornay was instantly recognisable as all that we once meant by South Kensington, that is near-smart, would-be up-to-date, inexpensively With It. Her clothes, like her slang, were last season's and she clanked with handmade peasant jewellery. Her voice was unnaturally cultured and everything about her, complexion, manicure, movement, was just off-elegant. Her hair had been done according to the mode of the moment but by 'a clever little woman down the road', and one felt that she knew a dozen such in each of the luxury trades. 'You can't tell the difference' might have been her motto. But you could.

Carolus rather vaguely explained himself but Mrs de Mornay at once asked him in.

'I've got the place to myself now,' she explained. 'Biskett the chauffeur looks in from time to time; otherwise the house is empty.'

'Miss Trudge has gone?'

'With the wind,' said Mrs de Mornay. 'Mr Smithers gave

her a month's wages and told her to move out. I'm staying on as long as he wants me.'

There was a suggestion of fervour about this remark. Carolus caught it and wondered.

'As a matter of fact,' added Mrs de Mornay, 'I may stay on altogether.'

She did not enlarge on this and Carolus enquired no further.

The house was, of course, a nightmare of modern *décor*, a set constructed for a film called *The Charm of Living* or some such thing. Invited to sit down Carolus occupied a bucket seat designed to resemble a giant inverted lemon with its centre cut out, and faced Mrs de Mornay squatting on a white toadstool with white-spotted scarlet upholstered top.

'Not *my* idea of a cosy little home,' Mrs de Mornay informed him. 'But you know what Genie *was*. You should see the kitchen. She collected gadgets, you see. Now, what is it you want to know?'

'Well, I wondered . . .'

'You think she was murdered, I take it, or you wouldn't be here. I shouldn't be surprised, myself. Have you met her sister?'

'Yes.'

'We've had a lot of trouble with her. She came here as soon as she was back from the country and started claiming good-ness-knows-what among Genie's things. I had to tell her plainly that Mr Smithers had given orders that nothing was to be touched. "But these are mine!" she said and I told her it didn't make any difference—they would stay here till Mr Smithers settled everything. In the end I had to ask her to leave. So you think Genie was murdered?'

'I...'

'Could be. A lot of people loathed her. Extraordinary woman really. I quite liked her though I never put up with any of her nonsense. She couldn't do without me and she knew it. I let her go so far and no farther. She never tried to treat me as she did the wretched Trudge.'

'Tell me about...'

'Trudge? She had no will of her own, poor old soul. She used to be very thick with Grace Marvell. But that ended in a blazing row about three months ago. It surprised me. I never thought Maud had it in her. They shouted at one another like fishwives. Genie was out at the time, fortunately. They didn't speak for a week after that and they've never been more than barely civil since it happened.'

'And Mr...'

'Smithers? He appeared about the same time, or a little before. I'd never seen him till then. He had refused to live with Genie. Can you wonder? He's a gentleman. I could tell that from the way he treated me. But I never knew what was between him and Genie till I heard about her will. I must say I was delighted. The first thing he did was to let me know that I shouldn't be the loser by it. He has that calm way of understanding things. You know him well, of course?'

'I've just...'

'But you can see he's a gentleman. I could, as soon as he came here. It surprised me, I must say. I wondered what on earth had made him marry Genie. They seemed to have nothing in common. But I suppose that was before she began her Career.'

'So you didn't know...'

'About the will? Not a thing until he told me. Grace talks

of disputing it but she hasn't a leg to stand on. She'll only waste what money she has if she tries.'

'And Miss . . .'

'Trudge? Not a hope. Though she really worked for Genie. She did most of the writing, you know. She must have made up recipes in her sleep. Genie couldn't even spell—in French or English. Trudge spoke good French and could type like lightning. But Genie knew what she was doing.'

'There had been another will . . .'

'Before the one leaving everything to Mr Smithers? Oh yes. Grace and Trudge were both in it. In fact I think almost everything went to them. They never knew they had been cut out—I'm sure of that. It must have come as a nasty shock to them.'

Carolus made a determined effort to put in a question.

'Mrs de Mornay, have you any reason . . .'

'To complain? Oh no. Mr Smithers . . .'

'I wasn't going to ask you that,' said Carolus loudly and with determination. 'Had you any reason to think Miss Marvell . . .'

'Was going to cut them out? Not a bit.'

'To think that Miss Marvell was ever threatened by any-one?' Carolus finished his question triumphantly. It actually silenced Mrs de Mornay for a moment.

'Threatened? Who by?'

'Anyone.'

'I never heard . . . She never said anything.'

'But was there anything to suggest it?'

'Not so far as I know. She wasn't the sort of woman to be threatened. I think if there had been anything like that she would have told me. Why? Do you think she was?'

'Have you ever heard the name Mandeville?'

'Isn't there a writer? I seem to remember . . .'

'I do not mean Sir John Mandeville. Nor Bernard de Mandeville. This man is alive today and uses that name.'

Mrs de Mornay shrugged.

'I've never heard of him,' she said. 'But that means nothing. I'm a fool about names.'

'You might have heard of someone known as Maxie? Does that ring a bell?'

'Of course! Maxie Miller.'

'I'm not thinking of the comedian.'

'Don't remember any other Max or Maxie. Beerbohm, of course, and Aitken, but don't suppose you mean those.'

'I don't. What about Rivers? No? Gray then?'

'Oh I know lots of Grays. Dorian, for example. And the Elegy man.'

'Not, in that sense, the Elegy man. This one is nicknamed "Razor" Gray.'

'How very unpleasant. Am I supposed to know him?'

'I'm just asking you.'

'I'm afraid there is no Razor Gray on my list of acquaintances,' said Mrs de Mornay with heavy sarcasm.

'Or Montreith?'

'No. Definitely.'

Carolus had waited for that word. It *had* to be a favourite of Mrs de Mornay's.

'Did Imogen Marvell confide in you much?'

'Yes. But not everything. She was rather secretive in some ways. Food was a common topic, of course. It had to be with Genie.'

'Did she . . . ?'

'Know anything about it? Not really. She had learned the patter and could turn a menu inside out . . .'

Emboldened by recent success, Carolus interrupted.

'Were her restaurants successful?'

'Oh yes. She used to print a recipe for each of the dishes served. That was her gimmick. She . . .'

'How far was she concerned with the actual running of them? On the spot, I mean?'

'Very little. Grace managed one. She had someone responsible in charge of each. She kept in touch by telephone. You should have seen her lying in her Spanish rococo bed, smothered in lingerie and swansdown, phoning to tell Grace or someone she was a silly bitch. Her language was just crude—not picturesque or funny, just four-letter words. Especially to those she employed.'

'It's not an attractive picture,' reflected Carolus. 'And nothing happened, nothing that you noticed during these recent weeks, to suggest that any kind of threat was being made to her connected with the restaurants?'

Mrs de Mornay fidgeted with her ponderous beads.

'She said she had a good mind to sell the lot of them—but she often said that. I don't think she ever would have, though. It was the only way she could ever see her name in lights— Imogen Marvell's Ma Façon Restaurant.'

'Did she keep a directory of private telephone numbers?'

'Trudge kept one for her. But it disappeared when Trudge did. We couldn't watch everything.'

'Who are "we"?'

'Mr Smithers and I.'

'Is Mr Smithers thinking of closing this house?'

'Closing it? Certainly not. He . . . we . . . I . . . It's a matter

I'm not at liberty to discuss at present.' There was a suggestion of coyness in Mrs de Mornay's manner. 'You see . . . But no doubt . . .'

This time Carolus's interruption was welcomed.

'Mrs de Mornay,' he said resolutely. 'The proprietors of a number of well-known restaurants have been the victims of organised blackmail recently. They are very vulnerable to this. A case of food poisoning, induced or imaginary, is enough to damage them and there are other means of attack. I realise that you had no direct connection with Imogen Marvell's restaurants but you knew her pretty well. Can you give me any help here?'

Mrs de Mornay gasped.

'You mean, they were blackmailing Imogen?' she said incredulously.

'I don't know. I . . .'

Carolus had lost the initiative again.

'That would be the *end*!' said Mrs de Mornay. 'Genie paying protection money. But you must be joking. If there was one thing Genie wouldn't pay it was money. Compliments, yes. Attention, yes, if it served her purpose. She could pay *out* too, in the sense of vengeance. But not money. You're barking up the wrong tree.'

Carolus was silent a moment as though wondering how much to say.

'The proprietor of the Fleur-de-Lys in which Imogen Marvell died was being blackmailed,' he said and allowed it to sink in.

'You think Genie's death was part of the plot? Well, that's a new one. She wouldn't have been madly pleased about that. To be killed just as a piece of stage "business" by a blackmailer.

I should have thought it was far more likely that she was *in* with the blackmailers.'

'You would?'

'Yes. Genie would have been at the receiving end of any hush money there was about.'

Carolus nodded and asked Mrs de Mornay whether he could see the chauffeur.

'Biskett? Of course you may if he's in the house. He's probably got some young woman with him. I'll find out.'

She left Carolus and returned to say that Biskett would be pleased to see him. Mrs de Mornay explained that he had a flat built on to the back of the house and was there now. Carolus went down.

An atmosphere of tobacco smoke and gin cleared sufficiently for Carolus to recognise Biskett, no longer wearing a cherry-coloured uniform but in an expensive suit. On the floor was kneeling a limp-looking girl with lank blonde hair hanging over her eyes.

'I rather hoped to see you alone for a minute,' said Carolus to Biskett when they had greeted one another civilly.

'Of course. Sonia, love, go and have a bath, will you?'

'But I've just had a bath, Dickie,' piped the blonde.

'Well, have another, sweet. Run along, because Dickie has to talk business with this gentleman.'

'I don't really want...'

'*Go and have a bath!*' shouted Biskett and the blonde disappeared. 'Now?' he said to Carolus.

Carolus gave rather more convincing reasons for his enquiries than he had hitherto done. Biskett was no fool, he decided as the young man watched him closely with green-grey eyes.

'You knew Imogen Marvell pretty well?' Carolus suggested.

'Scarcely at all. I kept it on a strictly business basis. Had to, with Imogen.'

'But you often drove her alone?'

'Not so often as you'd think. Trudge was usually with her.'

'But sometimes?'

'Occasionally, yes.'

'Anywhere particularly?'

'Not really. To one of her restaurants. Wine tastings. That sort of thing.'

'She apparently saw her lawyer without the knowledge of anyone in this house.'

'When was that?'

'About three months ago.'

'Oh yes. I remember. I brought him here. She sent Trudge and de Mornay out together to eat at a new restaurant. She evidently wanted them out of the way. They were to make a full report. As soon as they were gone she sent me with the car to pick up this solicitor character.'

'Where did you meet him?'

'At his offices in the Haymarket. He was standing in the doorway and as soon as he saw the car he came out and jumped in. There's one thing about that Rolls, you can't miss it. I brought him here and he was with Imogen for an hour. A few days later I took her to the office. That any help to you?'

'Yes. Thanks.'

They were interrupted by a call from the bathroom.

'Dickie! I've finished my bath!'

'Have another, then,' shouted Biskett.

Carolus went on to ask questions similar to those he had put to Mrs de Mornay and with no more result. Biskett had never seen or heard anything to make him think that Imogen Marvell was being threatened and considered it highly improbable. He had never heard the names Mandeville, Maxie, Rivers, Gray, or Montreith in connection with Imogen Marvell, though he *had* known a girl called Pamela Rivers.

'A model,' he said unenthusiastically. 'All legs and nothing at the top of them. I don't suppose she had anything to do with it.'

'It's a common name,' Carolus agreed.

There was another call from the bathroom.

'I'm coming out now!'

'Are you dressed?'

'No!'

'Then get dressed.'

'Shan't!'

'Don't, then. You're being a bore, Gladiola.' Biskett turned to Carolus. 'Anything else you wanted to know?'

'Yes. Did you ever drive Imogen Marvell to a block of flats in Bayswater called Gaitskell Mansions?'

He watched the chauffeur keenly as he answered but the negative was casual and convincing.

'No. I should have remembered the name.'

Carolus took his leave, observing as he did so that the bathroom door was ajar.

'What hell women are,' observed Dickie Biskett unconvincingly.

Fourteen

Back at the Fleur-de-Lys that evening Carolus found Gloria Gee in a state of anxiety and some excitement.

'It's about Tom Bridger,' she said, and looked at Carolus as though wondering whether he would be sympathetic.

'Well, Gloria?'

All Gloria's elocution practice went by the board.

'He's gorn!' she said, and Carolus could see that she was holding back her tears.

'You mean, left his job?'

'He didn't want to. I know *that*. He got a phone call. Then he came in here as white as a sheet. Honestly, you should have seen him, Mr Deene. I said "Whatever's the matter, Tom? You look as though you'd seen a ghost." "Perhaps I have," he said. Then he told me he'd got to go to London and was going to borrow Antoine's car. It's a Vauxhall.'

'Did Antoine lend it?'

'Oh yes. He's very good, like that.'

'Did Bridger take any baggage with him?'

'Not that I know of. No, I'm sure he didn't because Mrs Boot told me nothing had gone from his room. He just popped in here and said he was off to London and would be back that night.'

'When was this?'

'Yesterday afternoon. And there's nothing been heard of him since. What do you think it means?'

'It's very early to say, isn't it?'

'I *feel* there's something wrong. Honestly, Mr Deene, I have some queer instincts about people. My mother used to say I had second sight. As soon as Tom told me he was rushing off like that I knew there was something wrong. He looked scared.'

'Did he mean a lot to you, Gloria?'

'Well. You know. I suppose he did, in a way. He was such a cheerful fellow, wasn't he? I mean, I don't mean I was *mad* about him. But you know. I seemed to get used to him. He was ever so nice when my mum died.'

'Perhaps he'll turn up today.'

'I wish I could think so. Where do you think he's gone, any-way? He never told me he knew anyone particular in London.'

'Had he got a passport?'

'A passport? You mean you think he's gone off abroad? He wouldn't do that. Not without telling me. And what about all his things? Besides, he hadn't got a passport. He happened to mention it to me. We'd thought of going abroad together this summer. Spain, he said. The Coster something-or-other. Tom said he'd never been abroad and would have to get a passport.'

'I see. I may be able to find him. But don't count on it. I'm going to London myself tomorrow. Meanwhile I must see Rolland.'

He found the proprietor of the Fleur-de-Lys annoyingly cock-a-hoop.

'I'm glad I didn't give in to them,' he said.

'Why?'

'They've packed in. They've had it. The whole thing failed. I got more publicity from the fact that Imogen Marvell was buried from here than I've ever had. The restaurant's been packed.'

'You think they'll leave it at that?'

'What else can they do? They can see I'm not a man to be messed about. Besides, they've called in Bridger. You didn't realise this, but Bridger was obviously their man. It was he who worked the food poisoning—I can see it all now. And yesterday afternoon they phoned him to pull out of here.'

'How do you know?'

'What else can it have been? He had a phone call from London and rushed off at once in Antoine's car. Didn't even wait to pack his gear. They know when they're beaten.'

'I shouldn't be too sure, if I were you.'

Rolland's confidence was slightly shaken.

'Why do you say that?' he asked.

'I don't think these people give up easily. They can't afford to. They must either go on till they've won or lose their means of livelihood. They mustn't fail in one single case or they fail altogether.'

'Then what do you suppose they'll do?'

'If you want my advice, Rolland, you'll go to the police. Now. If you haven't the guts for that get yourself a bodyguard.'

Rolland stared.

'And what are *you* doing meanwhile? You're supposed to be trying to break these people, and you calmly talk about my getting a bodyguard. What do you intend to do?'

Carolus smiled.

'Put my head in the lion's mouth, perhaps. But it won't be to save *you* money.'

'I see. You're prepared to let them . . . beat me up. Perhaps . . .'

'Kill you? Not if I can prevent it. You, or anyone else. I detest this thing more than you. I'm going to fight it. But you don't make it any easier for me.'

'I've got my business to think of.'

'That's what you all say. You and the rest of them who have suffered from this. If it was just your businesses that are involved I half believe I'd drop it. But it's more than that.'

'What?'

'Murder,' said Carolus.

'What murder?'

'Possibly in the past, probably in the present, certainly in the future.'

'I see,' said Rolland looking very much less comfortable. 'And what exactly do you intend to do about it?'

'I'm going to see the man they call the boss.'

Rolland gave a forced laugh.

'How?'

'He's a solicitor. I'm going to consult him.'

'Really? On what?'

'On the case of a missing man. Bridger.'

Rolland started.

'Don't bring *me* into this!' he said. 'If you want to throw your life away by going to these people, you can. Though I don't see what you'll gain by it except to be beaten up and possibly worse.'

'I hope to gain information,' said Carolus mildly.

'Don't forget you're not acting for me.'

'Or anyone else. I'm on my own. You won't have to make any statement until you're quite, quite safe, Rolland. Now, where will I find Antoine?'

'In the kitchen. And very busy, with Bridger away. I hope you won't waste his time.'

Carolus found Antoine in the act of garnishing a lobster Newburg.

'Yes?' said the *chef* sulkily.

Carolus came to the point.

'Did you lend Bridger your car?'

'Yes.'

'Have you done so before?'

'Yes.'

'What is its make and index number?'

'Vauxhall. Victor Estate. Four months old. Pale blue. YYY808.'

'Thank you very much.'

Antoine nodded and became even more absorbed in his work. Carolus left.

Before going to bed that night he telephoned to his friend John Moore. John had been a young Detective Sergeant in Newminster when Carolus had first met him and had now climbed almost to the top of his profession as Detective Superintendent at Scotland Yard. The two men had remained friends but Moore was strictly a professional and was not to be drawn into Carolus's unconventional investigations except when his duty, rigidly interpreted, caused him to be. On this occasion Carolus did no more than ask if he could come and see him at his office tomorrow at 11.30. Moore agreed.

Then Carolus dialled the number of Mr Gorringer, his headmaster, and a muffled voice replied: 'Residence of the headmaster, Queen's School, Newminster.'

Carolus, who knew Mr Gorringer's penchant for making

himself difficult of access, said cheerfully: 'That you, head-master? Deene speaking.'

There was a pause in which Mr Gorringer could almost be heard debating in his mind whether to continue his impersonation or admit his identity. He decided, reluctantly, on the latter.

'Ah, Deene,' he said.

'I wondered whether by chance you would be in town tomorrow,' said Carolus. 'If so I hoped perhaps you would lunch with me.'

'It happens that I had intended to run up to London for an hour or two tomorrow,' said Mr Gorringer. 'I shall be somewhat occupied with school affairs but I have as yet made no luncheon appointment. I should be pleased to accept your invitation. Perhaps you will name the *venue?*'

Carolus, in view of the last weeks, chose a restaurant where there was no affectation of *haute cuisine,* which appeared in no list of recommended places to eat with starry grading, where the cook was probably called Bert and the food was extremely good.

'The Saddle of Lamb in Whitehall, at one o'clock?' he suggested.

'Excellent,' agreed Mr Gorringer. 'It is hard by my club, the United Headmasters and Headmistresses, where I already have an appointment during the morning.'

On the completion of these arrangements Carolus slept well and woke to find Mrs Boot in his room with a tea-tray.

'I heard it was you in here,' she said, 'and I knew you wouldn't want those Arabians creeping about when you woke up.'

'Thank you,' said Carolus.

'Specially after what's happened with them. You heard about that I suppose? Trying to kill one another. Dancing round the yard, they were. Pushing and making as though to strangle one another. Getting hold of each other's hair and kicking. Shouting all the time like a pair of lunatics. If they want to fight why can't they fight and have done with it? Then afterwards looking daggers at one another. Now they're thick as thieves again. I said to my husband, I feel as though I was in a menagerie, I said.'

Carolus made a sympathetic noise.

'Then there's that Gloria,' said Mrs Boot, 'crying her eyes out morning, noon and night because that Bridger's gone off somewhere. Mind you, there's something funny about that. I happened to be passing the phone box when he was in there and couldn't help hearing. "I never said anything," he kept saying. "He never heard anything from me." Then something about the Old Cygnet which he hadn't mentioned. I couldn't follow it all but I could see he was upset. Still, why she should blubber about it I can't think. It's not as though he's any loss, always grinning. I told Gloria. "Let him pop off if he wants to. There's plenty more," I said. But she wouldn't have it. There's some like that, aren't there?'

'I suppose there are. You actually overheard Bridger on the telephone?'

'I couldn't help it, could I? I'm not one to listen to anyone's conversation but he hadn't shut the door properly and I happened to be dusting just near.'

'What else did he say?'

'Nothing to speak of, really. He promised to go up somewhere or other that afternoon. He sounded as though he was upset, as I told you. And he went straight off for a drink afterwards. Then to Antoine to borrow his car. There was more in *that* than meets the eye. You don't find someone like Antoine lending a new car for nothing, do you? It's not as though the two of them were all that friendly. Antoine isn't one to give anything away. As soon as I saw what had happened I said to myself, that's funny, I said, Antoine lending his car like that. I wonder what he gets out of it. But there you are. You never know, do you?'

'No.'

'You'd never think that Gloria would give herself away like that, would you? It shows what there was between them and I've always said. You'd think she'd have more respect for herself than to show everyone. Still, there you are. As for that Stefan . . .'

'What's the matter with Stefan?'

'You know very well what's the matter with him. *Drink.* That's what's the matter with him. I don't see it so much because I'm not here at night. Though last night Mr Rolland asked me to come back because Bridger wasn't there and they needed help in the kitchen. I give you my word he could hardly stand up straight. How he went round the tables I don't know but I suppose he's used to it. Fancy a head waiter, though! You'd think he'd set an example, wouldn't you? I'd like to know where he keeps it. He doesn't often go in the bar. He doesn't get on with that Gloria if the truth were known. He seems to have been worse since all this happened, as though there was something on his mind. I think he knows more than what he's said. That's what it looks like, anyway.

'As for that Rolland, he's like a dog with two tails. You'd think he'd be at his wits' end with all this food poisoning and people being suffercated and Bridger going off, wouldn't you?

Not him. He was humming as he came through the hall this morning. You can hum, I said to myself, but what's going to happen next, that's what I want to know. And that Molt's been acting funny.'

'Funny?'

'Very funny. Going about with a face like a funeral and watching everyone out of the corner of his eye as though he thought a policeman was after him. If I hadn't worked here all these years I'd go, I can tell you. It was different in Mist'ran Misses Cheeseman's time. You didn't have all this going on. I don't say they wasn't close. She used to count the pickled eggs in the Public and write it down on a piece of paper. But we never had any Arabians here in their time—that was one thing. I should like to have seen Mist'ran Misses Cheeseman's faces if there'd been Arabians slinking round while they was here. Or if young Dave Paton was to have asked for more wages as he did yesterday.'

'Really?'

'I'm telling you, aren't I? Soon as ever Bridger didn't come back he was in the office saying he had twice the work to do and wanted more money. What's more, Rolland gave it him. Well, he had to, didn't he? It's a job to get anyone, nowadays. Well. This'll never do. I've got my work to see to. I can't stop here all day. Only I was going to tell you about that Dr Jyves.'

'Yes?'

'It's only what I've heard, mind you. I can't answer for it. But if half of it's true it's enough to make anyone think twice about being on his panel. It seems he's gone to pieces altogether. Doesn't seem to remember what he told you five minutes ago. Forgets where he is sometimes. They say it's drugs. But it may

144

be all talk. There's people in this place that are only too ready to take your character away from you. Going round saying things about one another. It's all wrong, isn't it?'

'It is.'

'I say to them sometimes, "Can't you say something good about people? If not, I don't know why you have to talk at all. We only live once. We might as well make the best of it." I do hate backbiting and making mischief. My husband's the same. He tries to make the best of everyone even if he knows what they are.

'Well. I must fly. I've got my staircase to do. They'll start wondering whatever's happened. They know I'm not one to stop gossiping when there's work to be done. Not like some of them I could mention. I asked them the other day. "Haven't you anything to do?" I said. They didn't half give me a look. They don't like anyone to call attention, do they?'

As though with a supreme effort, Mrs Boot made her exit.

Fifteen

Carolus was punctual in his call at John Moore's office. The Detective Superintendent gave the impression that delighted though he would be to see Carolus anywhere else on other business he had certain professional reserves about him at this time and in this place.

They exchanged warm greetings and enquiries. Then John Moore said, 'What can I do for you, Carolus? Because I know you too well to suppose you've come here to enquire after the wife and children.'

Carolus resisted the temptation to say it was a question of what *he* could do for Moore. He came straight to the point.

'What do you know about a firm working the protection racket on luxury restaurants and clubs?'

John Moore looked up sharply.

'You know it's not the slightest good your asking questions like that. Whatever we know, or don't know, I can't discuss that with you.'

'From which I take it that *one* you know something but not much, *two* that someone else is handling the matter, and *three* that it's giving you all a headache.'

John Moore sighed pointedly.

'I know enough to tell you to keep out of this, Carolus. What-

146

ever it is you can only do more harm than good to yourself and to us.'

'Unfortunately I'm too far involved.'

'Speaking generally—and it's the only way I can speak—the kind of case you describe is notoriously tricky. Months of work usually go to it as recent cases show. With exact knowledge of what's going on it may take anything up to a year before we can prosecute. And if some interfering outsider like you pushes in it may cause us trouble and delay. I tell you to get out of it, Carolus, and stay out.'

Carolus seemed to consider.

'Months, you say. Suppose it can be speeded up?'

'What do you mean by speeded up?'

'Suppose you were informed by some interfering outsider like me exactly who was running the thing and from what address? Also the names, or assumed names, of his assistants? Plus three of the people who are being blackmailed, or paying protection money if you like. What then, John?'

'It wouldn't necessarily alter the immediate position. The names may already be known. The identities of those being blackmailed are useless if they're afraid to give information. I am speaking in general terms of course.'

Carolus smiled.

'Of course,' he agreed. 'But suppose we carry the hypothesis a little further. Suppose that circumstances enabled you, indeed forced you, to arrest most or all of the principals on another charge on which bail would not be allowed. What then? Couldn't you get your information easily enough?'

'*What* circumstances?' asked John Moore.

'Suppose you found these people *in flagrante delicto,* with beaten-up victims actually on the premises? That would enable you to search . . .'

'Without a warrant?'

'Oh come, my dear John. Your memory must be short. The late Maxwell Fyfe, when as Home Secretary he caused to be circulated a directive ordering a drive against homosexuals, had to defend in the Commons the conduct of the police. He was asked on what authority they had searched the home of one of the victims of his prejudices. He said that since the man had been arrested *no search warrant was necessary,* or words to that effect. Does not the same apply here?'

'I am not saying a search of the premises could not be made if the tenant or owner was under arrest. But I think this has gone far enough, Carolus. So many ifs and buts. I've warned you in the friendliest way to keep out of this thing. If it's anything like you suggest you're risking your life. I mean that. The sort of people you describe stop at nothing.'

Carolus lit a cheroot.

'I don't think so,' he said. 'I did not expect you to welcome my interference, as you call it, though you must be aware that I could tell you a great deal you don't already know. I know you are bound by all sorts of restrictions on the use of informers. Let me put it to you this way. If you received information at, say, between four and five this afternoon, that at such and such an address a certain individual was being held by force and probably maltreated, would you not have to act?'

'By "a certain individual" I presume you mean yourself.'

'Could be.'

'Of course we should have to act. Whatever it was. A patrol would be sent to the address at once with orders to investigate.'

'*And,* my dear John, if you had reason to think that the

148

matter was a serious one, leading to the breaking up of a very dangerous criminal clique of blackmailers, with possibly one or more murders thrown in, would it not perhaps be your duty to accompany the patrol yourself, with sufficient force for all eventualities? I speak in general terms, of course.'

It was John Moore's turn to smile.

'No comment,' he said.

'But my point is taken? Good. The only other provision I should like to make is this—will you in fact be in your office between four and five this afternoon?'

John Moore made some play of examining an engagement book.

'Yes. I shall,' he said.

'Is there a number through which you can be reached at once, with no delay at all?'

The Detective Superintendent wrote a number on a slip of paper and silently handed it across.

'Thank you,' said Carolus. 'And now perhaps—still in general terms—I can chatter away a few moments of your time. I should just like to mention an address in case it should happen to interest you.'

John Moore's attempt to look bored was not a success. Nor did Carolus mistake the notes he made for doodling.

'It's a solicitor's office,' Carolus went on. 'A certain Montreith. On the first floor of Gaitskell Mansions, Attlee Avenue, Bayswater. There is a porter called Humbledon who may have been bribed.'

Moore said nothing, but no one could have supposed he was not listening.

'Above the offices, on the second floor, there is a flat, also Montreith's. A metal staircase runs up to it from the offices.

I don't know who will be in the offices or flat but if Montreith is out no one will call you and we're back to square one. There may possibly be a character known as Razor Gray and another, Rivers or Maxie.'

Was there a suggestion of recognition of these names on Moore's would-be inscrutable face?

'And possibly a gentleman who chooses the name Mandeville. Perhaps others. I imagine you'll see nothing at first but a quiet solicitor's office. That's the cover.'

John Moore rose.

'Well, Carolus, it's nice to have seen you,' he said. 'Goodbye for now.'

For once Carolus allowed himself a colloquialism which normally he detested. 'Be seeing you,' he said.

In the foyer of the Saddle of Lamb Mr Gorringer was already waiting. His gift for making his presence felt in all surroundings was evident. His mighty red ears, hairy at the orifice, his weightiness and height, his protuberant eyes were all too noticeable.

'Ah, Deene,' he said. 'This is indeed a pleasure. As you know I all too rarely leave our academic backwater for the stir and bustle of the metropolis.'

'I hope I am not late, headmaster?'

'Not in the least. I have been filling the unforgiving minute with observation.'

'Have a drink before we go in to lunch?'

Mr Gorringer inclined his head.

'I should appreciate a glass of sherry,' he admitted. 'Are we to celebrate some new triumph of yours in the field of your curious hobby?'

'Not yet, I'm afraid.'

'You are not, I trust, still engaged in some investigation or other? I must remind you that our term starts in two days' time.'

'That's just why I've asked you to meet me, headmaster. I need your help.'

'My help? Only, I trust, in extricating you from circumstances irrelevant to our educational work?'

'You can call it that.'

'May I ask what is the nature of the assistance I can render you? As you know, my dear Deene, the welfare of my staff lies very close to my heart. Only last week I was called upon to arrange a small advance for one of them whose wife is expecting to . . .'

'Not Hollingbourne again? This will be the sixth.'

'I name no names. I was merely demonstrating my willingness, in cases of real necessity, to go to the assistance of those who loyally serve the school. Though I am confident that your problem is not of that nature.'

'No, headmaster. It is not. Shall we have lunch? I will tell you while we eat.'

'An excellent idea. Let us be fortified against any dire eventuality.'

When they had ordered, Mr Gorringer leaving the details to Carolus, the headmaster prepared to listen.

'I am all ears,' he said with small exaggeration.

'Do you happen to be free about four o'clock this afternoon?'

'I shall have completed my business by then, I trust. I intended to catch a train for Newminster at 5.7.'

'Would you oblige me by coming to Bayswater?'

'Bayswater, my dear Deene? A most reputable district, I

believe. I have no objection to accompanying you to Bayswater. But what is the nature of the service I can render you there?'

'Just to make a phone call. From a public box.'

Mr Gorringer considered.

'I cannot help but feel, my dear Deene, that such a task could be undertaken by any of your numerous acquaintances. It seems scarcely necessary to ask your headmaster.'

'It's a matter of life and death,' said Carolus shortly.

'In that case,' said Mr Gorringer, 'I should require to be informed of the circumstances.'

'Yes,' said Carolus. 'I see that.'

He proceeded to recount the events at the Fleur-de-Lys with frankness while Mr Gorringer ate and listened. Then he waited for the headmaster's pronouncements.

'It seems,' said Mr Gorringer, 'a most distasteful affair. Blackmail, protection, extortion, possibly murder, these are scarcely suitable as the concern of the senior history master at Queen's School, Newminster. Nevertheless, as you outline the case I see that once having involved yourself you have acted with courage and determination. I cannot criticise your conduct on that score. But the question remains, Deene. Where will this end?'

'In Bayswater. This afternoon.'

Carolus went on to tell him of his call on John Moore and the upshot of it.

'I have come to you,' he added, 'because as you will see, I need help from someone I can count on absolutely. I know it is an imposition. But that phone call really may be a matter of life and death. These people stop at nothing.'

Mr Gorringer looked more solemn than ever.

'Since you put it like that,' he said, 'you leave me no alternative. I scarcely supposed when I accepted this headmastership that it would involve me in acting to protect the physical security, possibly the life of one of my assistants from the violence of a dangerous gang of thugs. I scarcely imagined that I would be called on to travel to Bayswater to rescue a colleague threatened by criminals. But—*tout comprendre est tout pardonner*. You have explained the matter frankly and I do not see how I can refuse. Please outline the plan of action.'

'We will go there in a taxi. There is a public call box in the same street. If when we drive up it is occupied we shall have to drive about until it is free. When it is, the taxi will stop and you will go into the box where you will appear to be in conversation for five full minutes. Should anyone show impatience for the use of the box you will ignore it. It is essential that you keep possession of it for that time.'

Mr Gorringer seemed already to be rehearsing in his mind. 'So much I can undertake,' he said solemnly.

'Meanwhile you will keep your eye on the entrance to Gaitskell Mansions. If I come out during those five minutes it will mean that I have been unable to get into Montreith's offices and the whole operation will have to be abandoned or postponed. If I don't come out you will call this number.' He gave him Moore's. 'Ask for Detective Superintendent John Moore. He will probably answer the phone himself.'

'Shall I reveal my identity?' enquired Mr Gorringer with the air of a conspirator.

'No need to. Simply tell him . . .'

'But,' interrupted Mr Gorringer, 'it would surely add weight to what I shall tell him if he was aware that the head-master of the Queen's School himself was speaking?'

'He's prepared for this call. All you have to tell him is that you have reason to think that a man is being forcibly held in the offices of a solicitor named Montreith in Gaitskell Mansions, Attlee Avenue, Bayswater. He will act on that. You will have rendered me a great service, headmaster, and may still be able to catch the 5.7.'

'You don't think that any disguise will be necessary, Deene?'

'Disguise? What for?'

'I need scarcely tell you that my features are familiar to a wide public concerned with education. The people against whom we are taking these steps may well recognise them. Nothing must be done which could in any way involve me or the school in this affair. You should surely be the first to realise that?'

'You won't be involved.'

'My role ends with the telephone call? You do not think it would be wise for me to remain on the spot to render assistance, if necessary, at a later stage?'

'I don't. I think it would be most unwise.'

'Yet I would not have it thought that I abandoned a sinking ship. Like the immortal Macbeth, "I dare do all that may become a man; who dares do more is none." '

'I know. I appreciate it. But I assure you that you should not hang about.'

'It is true that Mrs Gorringer is expecting me on the 5.7. And by the way, Deene, we will make no mention in Newminster of this episode. It might be found inconsistent with my status in the town. You appreciate that, I am sure.'

'Certainly.'

'Then let us prepare ourselves for the ordeal. We go at once?'

'No. There is something I have to do first in Bayswater. Perhaps we could meet there?'

'Though it is not a region with which I am particularly familiar I believe that on its outskirts is to be found a department store familiar to me in childhood. In a word, Whiteley's. I will await you in the optical department of that store.'

'Why the optical department?'

'Despite your somewhat peremptory dismissal of my suggestions, Deene, I intend to take the elementary precaution of wearing a pair of tinted spectacles.'

'Say four o'clock, then?'

'Four o'clock it shall be.'

Sixteen

It took Carolus less time than he anticipated to find Antoine's light blue Vauxhall Victor Estate car number YYY808. It was in the subterranean parking place of a big garage some three hundred yards away from Gaitskell Mansions. He could, however, learn nothing about it from the busy staff of the place except the time and date on which it had been left and these exactly fitted with the time Bridger would have reached London if he had come straight to Attlee Avenue.

It was fair to assume that Bridger had gone to Montreith's offices. Either he had remained there or if he had emerged it was not with freedom to recover the car and drive away.

Reaching Whiteley's, Carolus found the optical department and was not surprised to see Mr Gorringer standing there resembling the store detective of fiction and the films. Carolus hurried him out and they were lucky to get a taxi from which some eager shoppers had alighted.

Carolus directed the taxi driver to Attlee Avenue.

'What part?' asked the driver.

'Would you just drive along it and I'll tell you?'

They found that the telephone booth was occupied by a woman.

'Unfortunate,' said Mr Gorringer. 'My experience of the conversational propensities of the other sex augurs ill.'

'Where to?' asked the taxi driver and Carolus described a circuit he could make.

'Joy riding, are you?' he said.

It was a relief to all of them when they returned to Attlee Avenue to see that the woman had gone. Mr Gorringer alighted with urgency and resolve and occupied the box. Telling the taxi driver to drive round the next corner, Carolus paid him liberally.

'Now I wonder what you two are up to,' the driver observed aloud. 'Would it be something to do with horse-racing? You get all sorts in my job so you can't help wondering, can you?'

'Yes,' said Carolus firmly and walked back to Attlee Avenue. He passed the telephone booth on the other side of the road and observed Mr Gorringer diligently in conversation while he watched the entrance to Gaitskell Mansions. Was he, Carolus wondered, reciting verses learned by heart as a schoolboy? Or repeating the names and dates of the kings of England? No one waited to use the booth so his efforts were art for art's sake.

At the entrance to Gaitskell Mansions Carolus ventured to turn and look across. He received a ponderous nod.

Humbledon was in the hallway and without actually barring Carolus's entry seemed to expect to be approached.

' 'Evening,' said Carolus. 'Mr Montreith in?'

Humbledon examined Carolus carefully.

'I'm not to know, am I? He might be or he might not.'

Carolus put a pound note in a palm already half extended.

'Haven't I seen you before?' Humbledon asked.

'Quite likely. Is Montreith in?'

'Yes. He's got two of them with him.' Humbledon's eyes suddenly widened to a stare. 'Aren't you the man that came that night when someone banged one of them on the head in the car? Didn't I show you out the back way?'

Carolus saw at once that this recognition, relayed to Montreith by telephone, would help him achieve his object.

'That's it,' he said.

'I shouldn't go up there then, if I was you.'

'I have to see Montreith.'

'I'm not saying any more. You go up there if you like. Only don't say I didn't tell you.'

Carolus moved towards the staircase. Even as he began to ascend he saw Humbledon enter his cubby-hole, doubtless to use the telephone.

On the first floor was the sign *Rowland Montreith, Solicitor. Enquiries.* It faced Carolus as he reached the wide landing. It was a neat sign, neither too large nor over-discreet. He rang the bell. There was a pause of a few minutes before Rivers opened the door. When he saw Carolus he gave his not quite inane laugh and said, 'Come in!'

Carolus did not ask to see Montreith and Rivers made no enquiry as to his business but showed him into a small waiting-room and left him.

Carolus was calculating time. To hasten things was dangerous for himself but delay here might mean the arrival of the police before he was ready.

He was about to walk in to the inner office when Rivers came back to say mirthfully: 'He'll see you now.'

There was nothing showy about Montreith or the room in which he sat at a plain, old-fashioned but not antique desk. He was wearing a dark-coloured suit with a plain dark tie, not elegant but not in the least shabby. Seeing him from close at hand Carolus judged his age as forty-two, but there was something seedy and unhealthy about him and he had a muddy and colourless complexion. It was, as Bridger had told him, the eyes which one noticed. 'Cold, nasty-looking,' Bridger had said. They were more than that, cruelly impassive, as far from smiling as the eyes of dead fish, of icy grey-green. He looked more composed and at the same time more dangerous than he had appeared in the Tourterelle.

At a smaller table on the right were two seats at which were Rivers and Gray, apparently occupied with books and papers.

No chair had been set for Carolus and no unoccupied chair was in the room. This, Carolus guessed, was by design. He promptly went up and sat on the corner of Montreith's table.

Montreith, he judged, had remarkable control. Until he had heard what Carolus had to say and learned a great deal more about him, he did not lose his temper.

'Do you want a chair?' he asked frigidly.

'Of course I want a chair,' said Carolus.

'Give Mr Deene a chair,' said Montreith to Rivers.

Carolus noted, but did not remark on, Montreith's knowledge of his name.

'What can I do for you?' asked Montreith.

'I want to consult you. I understand you have a large criminal practice.'

Montreith watched him without changing his expression, but did not immediately answer. He was trying to decide what was the meaning of Carolus's intrusion. At last he said, 'Well?'

'I want to consult you in the matter of a man named Bridger,' said Carolus.

He was aware of stirrings from Rivers and a quick glance from Gray.

'Yes?' said Montreith.

'He was assistant *chef* at the Fleur-de-Lys at Farringforth.

But he was also the local representative, as it were, of a gang of petty blackmailers and thugs who were trying to extort money from a man named Rowlands or Rolland, the proprietor of the Fleur-de-Lys.'

'Oh yes?' said Montreith.

Time was passing dangerously.

'He has disappeared,' Carolus went on. 'He was called on the telephone to account for something he had revealed and summoned to London. He borrowed a motor-car and came up. He has not been heard of since.'

Montreith spoke at last. He had a harsh but somewhat high-pitched voice.

'You say this man was called to account for something he had revealed? Surely that would explain his disappearance.'

'Yes, but not his whereabouts.'

'And you have come to consult me on that?'

'Exactly.'

'What is your connection with this matter?'

'That of an incurably inquisitive man.'

'Curiosity, in fact? That's easily cured.'

'Not when it's tied up with a very strong prejudice against blackmail and murder.'

Montreith's expression did not change but again there were movements at the other table.

'Where is Bridger?' Carolus asked calmly.

'I wonder why you ask me that.'

'Because the car he borrowed is not far from this building.'

This caused a complete hush, an atmosphere of suspense in the room. In spite of the outward imperturbability of Montreith, Carolus felt that he was faced with the necessity of instantly reaching a decision. And that decision was—should he or should he not cause Carolus to be killed. As simple as that.

His next remark was so unexpected that Carolus had to suppress his amazement.

'I am looking for a partner,' he said, those cold fish eyes on Carolus. Again there was silence.

Suddenly there broke in on them the sound of the telephone and Montreith lifted the receiver.

Now he showed that his calm could snap. He jumped up.

'Get him out of here!' he almost shouted to Rivers and Gray.

'Quick. And stay out yourselves.'

The two came forward at once. Carolus gave very little resistance—this was what he wanted. Gray pinioned him and he was hurried across the floor of the room.

An electric bell sounded.

'The back room,' said Montreith.

Carolus was propelled through a door behind Montreith, across a passage and into a bare room. Yes, Bridger had been right. It was windowless.

Carolus continued to struggle weakly. He had learned enough of Montreith and his friends to be pretty sure these two would not act without their chief's authority, would in fact limit themselves to keeping him quiet and secure. But he wanted it to be clearly established that he was being detained against his will. He freed an arm for a moment and managed to land a blow on Gray's jaw.

He hoped they would produce rope, but apparently none was handy for Rivers pulled off a long knitted tie and secured Carolus's wrists.

Carolus raised a shout but was immediately gagged with a handkerchief. He then sat down.

The two men did not speak but Rivers lit a cigarette.

Carolus's mind worked fast. He thought of what could have misfired in his preparations. Gorringer, for all his absurd self-importance, was not likely to have failed in his mission, and John Moore had perfectly understood the situation and its dangers. Some wholly unforeseeable delay in getting here? Breakdowns could happen—even to a squad car. But what could have caused Montreith's moment of near panic if it was not Humbledon calling to tell him that the police where on their way up? It all seemed cast-iron, but without being melodramatic about it, Carolus knew that his life was not worth much if there had been the smallest slip-up. Or—scarcely conceivable—if Montreith succeeded in bluffing John Moore to leave the place without searching.

It seemed to Carolus at least five minutes before somebody from outside the room tried the handle of the door. Rivers had turned the key and now stood irresolute.

'Open it,' said Gray whose brain was quicker than his companion's. It would only have been a moment before the door would have been forced.

What seemed strange to Carolus, when he recalled it afterwards, was the comparative silence with which everyone moved. John Moore and two hefty followers entered the room and neither Gray nor Rivers resisted handcuffs. Then Moore removed Carolus's gag and pulled out an old-fashioned pocket-knife with which he cut the knitted tie. They then returned to the office where two men had remained with Montreith. He too was handcuffed.

'Sit down, you three,' Moore said, and nodded to one of his assistants, who left the room.

Carolus lit a cheroot but said nothing. This was Moore's

scene, however much Carolus might have done to bring it about. He realised that the two CID men were searching the premises and waited, as John Moore did, for them to report.

'Let's have a smoke,' said Gray. A policeman lit a cigarette for him.

It must have been five minutes before the two men returned to the office.

'There's a dead man upstairs,' one of them told Moore.

'Bridger,' said Carolus.

'See if you can identify him, will you, Mr Deene?'

Carolus noted the formality of this but followed one of the CID men from the room without speaking.

He led the way to another back office in which there was a spiral staircase of iron. They climbed this to another small room also rather bare though one wall was covered with tightly filled bookshelves and the floor was thickly carpeted. As he crossed a landing Carolus had time to notice a Sheraton table, a painting by Francis Bacon and more books in eighteenth-century bindings.

They entered a large bedroom, large enough to make an immense Jacobean four-poster bed stand without appearing to fill the area. On it was a man, his face turned away. He looked as though he had thrown himself down in his clothes and gone to sleep.

Carolus walked round the bed and saw that the man was Bridger. The face had been brutally knocked about and was only just recognisable and the grin which had characterised Bridger in life now grotesquely stretched the lips.

'Strangled—or hanged,' the CID man said. 'Do you know him?'

'Yes. I can identify him.'

'Better come down to the Super then,' the CID man said placidly. 'We shall want his name for the charge sheet, probably. Though there's plenty more on which to hold this lot. We'll go down by the open staircase. I don't fancy climbing down that helter-skelter.'

As they did so they saw Humbledon hanging about on the landing.

'You can wait downstairs,' the CID man said briefly.

Carolus joined John Moore.

'I can identify the dead man. He has been working at the Fleur-de-Lys Hotel, Farringforth, as assistant *chef* under the name of Tom Bridger.'

'Anything more?'

'A car he borrowed on the day before yesterday from the *chef*, Vauxhall Victor YYY808, is in the Bevin Road Garage round the corner from here.'

'I should like you to come with me to make a statement,' said Moore, curtly, and Carolus nodded agreement.

'Get these into the van,' Moore ordered. 'I'll follow with Mr Deene. Leave two men here.'

Carolus was surprised that no protest came from Montreith. There was nothing of the traditional or mythical 'it's-a-fair-cop' in his attitude. His face remained expressionless, indeed he gave the impression of having anticipated these events and prepared for them. Of the three men the most visibly shaken was Rivers; his fleshy face had taken on a curious pallor.

Only when the whole group, but for two men in uniform, had left the room, did John Moore permit himself to give Carolus a grim smile.

But Carolus did not return it. He was wondering how far he was responsible for the death of Bridger.

Seventeen

On the following day, which was the eve of the new term at the Queen's School, Newminster, Carolus prepared to entertain John Moore and Mr Gorringer to dinner, after which he proposed to give them some account of his activities during the past weeks and explain any mystery that remained.

He found his housekeeper unexpectedly sympathetic to the project.

'As long as it's the headmaster coming,' she said, the clause serving her as an acquiescent sentence in itself.

'Yes. And Mr Moore. You remember him.'

'I'm not saying I don't,' said Mrs Stick cautiously. 'What were you thinking of giving them?'

'I leave that to you, Mrs Stick. Something simple. I've had so much pretentious food lately that I never want to see the word *scampi* again.'

Mrs Stick surprised him.

'How about a dozen Whitstable oysters, sirloin of Scotch beef with Yorkshire pudding and Stilton cheese?'

'What could be better?' asked Carolus, not altogether rhetorically.

The headmaster was the first to arrive.

'Ah, Deene,' he said, 'I made a point of coming early because I wanted a word with you. Is it your intention to reveal to the Detective Superintendent that it was your head-master who effected the crucial telephone call to his office?'

'Just as you like.'

'There is much to be said on both sides. While it would doubtless strengthen your case if he was made aware that the mysterious caller was none other than myself, it would be more than unfortunate if I were involved in the processes of the law which will follow. I should perhaps tell you that in addition to wearing a pair of shaded spectacles I felt it behoved me to assume a somewhat foreign accent in speaking to him. I gave the name of Chaminade, a lady composer of note I believe.'

'You did?'

'It will perhaps provide some wry amusement to a senior officer in the Criminal Investigation Department to know that he was so effectively misled.'

'I daresay it will.'

But when John Moore came breezily into the room and Carolus said, 'You know Mr Gorringer, of course?' he replied with a grin, 'Alias M. Chaminade, I think?'

Mr Gorringer took it in good part.

'I am delighted,' he announced, 'to find that a member of our excellent police force is so perspicacious.'

His good humour lasted throughout dinner, but when the three men had sunk into armchairs by the fire he spoke with more gravity.

'We must not forget,' he said, 'that a human life has been lost. While we have co-operated in the apprehension of a most dangerous gang of criminals on which we can certainly congratulate ourselves, there is this more sombre side of the picture. I hope that Deene will set our minds at rest.'

'I was very half-hearted about the case at first,' Carolus

recalled. 'I did not like Rolland or what he stood for. But blackmail is an abominable thing whoever suffers from it and, as I told Rolland, goes hand-in-glove with murder as often as not. My curiosity was roused too by the monstrous personality of Imogen Marvell and almost before I realised it I became involved.'

He described how he had concealed himself in the back of the car in which Rivers and Gray had driven to Montreith's offices and so discovered the headquarters of the gang.

He did not conceal from them that he had appropriated Rivers's wallet in the hope that it would produce information.

'While I am the first to realise that the criminal must be fought with his own weapons,' put in Mr Gorringer, 'I cannot but feel that the thought of my senior history master taking a wallet from the pocket of an unconscious man fills me with disquietude.'

'There wasn't a shred of information in it,' Carolus told him. 'Only seventeen pound notes which I dropped in the nearest Poor Box.'

Carolus went on to explain how he had first deduced from Dave Paton's story of having been sent by Bridger to speak to Mandeville that Bridger was in some way connected with the gang and wanted to divert suspicion from himself. This was confirmed when Mrs Boot told him he had been in conversation with Mandeville in the Spinning Wheel Café on the afternoon before Imogen Marvell died. 'I was sure enough to bluff Bridger into admitting to me that he had been responsible for Imogen Marvell's food poisoning,' said Carolus.

'But he told me something more valuable than that. I warned him that he could not trust me to keep him out of the thing, that I intended to report everything I knew. "You can only trust me not to let your friends know where I got the information," I remember saying. I stuck to that, but he didn't, poor wretch. Moreover I begged him to get away although his absence would have weakened my case. But he was broke and expecting money from Montreith, and foolishly stayed on.

'Mrs Boot heard the Old Cygnet Restaurant mentioned when Bridger was called from London, so I suppose it was the proprietor of this who told Montreith about my making enquiries. From that he guessed that Bridger had talked—but it was only a guess and if Bridger had kept his head he might have saved himself.

'Bridger tried to run with the hare and hunt with the hounds. He wasn't a brave man and on his first visit to Gaitskell Mansions they showed him someone who had been badly beaten up. He fell for that and once involved, accepting their offer of £100 for putting an emetic in the food, he left himself no escape. The first step in agreeing to take part in a conspiracy of that kind is the fatal one. From the moment he agreed to do what they wanted whatever the inducement or threat, he began walking to his death. I daresay, John, you will find there were others like him. His body was probably waiting to be taken away and put in an acid bath and if there have been other such disappearances the bodies were given the same treatment. But you know all that.'

'What I don't know from you,' said John Moore rather sternly, 'is—who are the two restaurant proprietors who have been paying protection money? You have mentioned the Old Cygnet. Was this one of them?'

Carolus told him about the John Bullish Mr Porter of the Old Cygnet and the more spirited Mr Leroy of the Tourterelle.

'They'll both talk,' he predicted. 'As soon as they know that Montreith, Rivers and Gray are charged with murder. Leroy actually promised me he would. And I'm sure they're not the only ones. You'll have them all running to you once the danger is removed. Gaming club owners, strip club proprietors, brothel owners (or those who live on immoral earnings, as we more politely call them), fruit machine owners, betting shops, bookmakers—Montreith's net was wide. I should not be in the least surprised if you found a few drug-carriers caught in it, importers of marihuana and the rest. I doubt if Montreith would have neglected such a lucrative source of income.'

'You mean . . .' Mr Gorringer sounded exultant. 'That we have not only smashed a gang of blackmailers and murderers but curtailed their activity in a more insidious form of crime, the dissemination of dangerous narcotics? We can indeed congratulate ourselves.'

Moore said nothing, but Carolus felt that he knew a good deal more than he was prepared to discuss.

'As for what the headmaster calls the gang of blackmailers and murderers, unless you, John, have been pretty busy today, as I expect you have, there must remain a number to take in. Montreith could not have achieved what he did without a good many free-lance bullies and extortioners, some of whom probably did not know for whom they were working. It is not difficult or expensive to have a rich man intimidated especially when in criminal terms there is something screwy about his business already. You will probably have a few thoroughly unpleasant thugs to put in the dock with Montreith.'

Moore nodded.

'As for the manner of Bridger's death, I prefer not to know details,' went on Carolus, 'though I daresay you have these by now. Or even whether there will be other murder charges. I know you can't answer questions but I should like to know whether the man who called himself Mandeville has been charged.'

'Oh yes,' said Moore. 'There's no secret about that. His name is Smith, as a matter of fact.'

Carolus asked no more.

'The character of Montreith interests me,' he said. 'Although the professional man who turns criminal is a favourite figure in novels and the outpourings of so-called crime reporters, he is still very rare in real life. I don't mean among young tearaways, but among serious and dedicated law-breakers. I should like to know how Montreith began, whether he was ever a seriously practising solicitor, and all the rest of it. He was self-indulgent —we know that—also cruel and vicious. What background did he come from? How did he start? How successful was he?'

'Doubtless you will know all in time,' suggested Mr Gorringer ponderously. 'Our national newspapers show no reluctance to provide us with details of the kind you mention. But there is another matter, my dear Deene, on which you have scarcely touched, and one I should have thought of considerable interest both to me and the Detective Superintendent. Namely, the untimely death of Miss Imogen Marvell.'

'Marvell? Oh, she was murdered, of course,' said Carolus off-handedly.

'You cannot be serious, Deene. A woman of world-wide reputation in the useful field of domestic science! An eminent authoress on gastronomical subjects! A household word in household management! Yet you suggest that she was murdered as though it were a commonplace. Where is your sense of proportion, man?'

'Murder is never a commonplace, headmaster, and I did not mean to suggest it, even of Imogen Marvell's murder.'

'Then please elucidate,' said Mr Gorringer. 'If this crime has been committed we—and the world—are entitled to the knowledge of who is guilty. Let him be put in the pillory, tried, and punished.'

'I doubt if there will ever be a trial or any punishment more than that being suffered already. I can produce no proof and no more than the most circumstantial of evidence. The coroner and presumably the police were satisfied that she died naturally. But for what it is worth I will tell you how I think it happened.

'She was, as you know, a woman who aroused much dislike —in fact hatred would not be too strong a word. Her success was as you say phenomenal and based on a flair for self-advertisement supported by the efforts of other people. Her sister claimed to have taught her all she knew about food, and her secretary, I have been told by her housekeeper, Mrs de Mornay, did most of her writing. Her husband and she had been separated for years and there were people in her profession who were bitterly jealous of her. Moreover, it seemed, as the informative Mrs Boot pointed out to me, that anyone on the spot could have been responsible for her death.

'There was a pretty collection of what are called suspects. Connected with the hotel there was Rolland himself, Anthony Brown known as Antoine the *chef,* Gloria Gee, Bridger, Stephen Digby, known as Stefan the head waiter, Dave Paton the apprentice, Ali and Abdul the Moroccan waiters, Molt, the wine waiter, and if you want to stretch possibilities to the farthest, Mrs Boot.

'Connected with Imogen Marvell there was her secretary,

Maud Trudge, her husband, Dudley Smithers, her sister, Grace Marvell, her chauffeur, Richard Biskett, and again stretching it perhaps, Dr Jyves.

'I use the word suspects in the conventional sense. I did not regard the majority of these people as even remotely suspect. But there were certain anomalous circumstances which, too late for action, aroused my curiosity.

'First of all the bitter enmity between Grace Marvell and Miss Trudge. I felt there was something excessive and not quite genuine about it. I first heard Grace Marvell speak of Miss Trudge's devotion to Imogen as "bitch-like". "I can't bear her," she told me, quite unnecessarily. Then Gloria Gee told me on Biskett's authority, "those two hate each other now though they were friendly enough till about three months ago." Again, when the question of an injection arose, Biskett reported that they "had the same thing with her about three months ago" and the same space of time had passed since the re-appearance of her husband Dudley Smithers. Finally, there was Mrs de Mornay's evidence on this point. "She (Miss Trudge) used to be very thick with Grace Marvell. But that ended in a blazing row about three months ago . . . They shouted at one another like fishwives." This surprised Mrs de Mornay who never thought Miss Trudge "had it in her."

'She was quite right, Miss Trudge hadn't. The quarrel was faked.'

Carolus paused, aware now of Moore's keen interest.

'If I had needed more evidence that the quarrel was pure stagecraft and make-believe, I had it when the contents of the will had been told them. If they had been genuinely at daggers drawn, Grace would never have rallied Trudge to fight the will *with* her, as she did. Each would have tried for herself.

But Grace, in the fury of the moment, showed that she and the secretary worked together. "We must do something. We're going to fight this thing tooth and nail", she said to Trudge.

'No, the quarrel was faked because it suited the purpose of these two women, who were both suffering under the heel of Imogen, and who believed (what until that time was true) that they would inherit everything on her death.'

'Purpose, Deene?' questioned Mr Gorringer. 'What purpose?'

'They decided to kill Imogen Marvell.'

'Good gracious me! Are you certain of what you say?'

'No. I'm not. I probably never shall be. I have warned you that the evidence is circumstantial. But my theory fits the facts, such as they are.

'Three months before she died, Imogen Marvell had one of her violent fits of hysteria and her doctor gave her an injection of Dormodina. Both Miss Trudge and Grace Marvell—who described the occasion—saw the effects of this. The doctor may even have warned them (as a doctor warned me on a similar occasion) of the very remote but none the less possible chance of suffocation during a sleep so induced. They were then "very thick", I was told. Suppose they decided that on the next occasion when Imogen was given such an injection they would make sure of that suffocation in a way that would not be detected.

'Their first step was to quarrel so that there could be no imputation of collaboration. They did not, Mrs de Mornay told me, speak to one another for a week after their noisy quarrel (so foreign to the nature of both), and had "never been more than barely civil since it happened".

'They had everything to gain. They knew that Imogen

Marvell had made a will in their favour and they did *not* know —Mrs de Mornay was sure of this—that the will had been changed. They were waiting for their chance.

'It came at the Fleur-de-Lys after Imogen had swallowed Bridger's emetic in the *scampi*. Imogen felt she had been made to look ridiculous both in the restaurant and in the press. She raved and Grace Marvell, playing her part, induced Dr Jyves to inject Dormodina.

'Then it was Maud Trudge's turn to act according to plan. She deliberately scratched her arm till blood came, implying by inventing foolish explanations that Imogen had done this in a fit of temper. Grace Marvell went for sticking-plaster and alcohol. These were necessary for their plan. Had they been in the luggage of any of them it might have aroused suspicion. So they purchased them openly in order to treat Miss Trudge's arm.

'Miss Trudge was the Macbeth of the conspiracy, needing Grace's support and determination to make her act. But she did so. She stayed with Imogen when the injection had been given and remained with her, or near at hand, until she felt sure that her deep Dormodina-induced sleep would continue through almost anything. She sealed her mouth with sticking-plaster, then her nose. The unfortunate woman probably struggled very little. Miss Trudge was equal to that. After a few spasmodic movements she died, and Miss Trudge could remove the plaster and with the alcohol all traces of the plaster. The acting of both women, born of despair and greed, was so good that it deceived me. It was not until Mrs de Mornay described them as shouting at one another like fishwives that I suspected the truth and the sticking-plaster and alcohol seemed to me evidence. Then it was too late.

'The timing of the actual murder is interesting. Dr Jyves gave Imogen the injection at about 9.10 and Trudge remained with her while Grace came downstairs. At 9.35 Stefan went to the room with a bottle of champagne which Imogen had ordered. He found the lights out and Imogen "snoring like a pig". Trudge may have been waiting in her own room until she thought Imogen would be fully under the effects of the drug, she may have gone into Imogen's bathroom. Stefan left the bottle. Trudge thereupon locked the door, one may suppose, and fortified with the champagne carried out her task. She rejoined us downstairs at 10.20. When Dudley Smithers looked in on his wife at 10.50 she was dead.

'What Trudge and Grace did nothing to simulate was their anger and dismay when they found that, purely to spite them it would seem, Imogen had left her fortune to her husband. That was genuine enough and will probably continue to the end of their lives. They have been punished certainly, but I do not think either of them will ever stand trial for murder. Unless...'

'Unless?' asked John Moore, breaking his long silence.

'Unless, by chance, the case is re-opened and an exhumation order is made and some trace of the sticking-plaster is found round Imogen's mouth or nose. All very unlikely. Or unless the two women fall out and are guilty of some wild indiscretion. Or Miss Trudge, less balanced than her co-conspirator, does something mad about it. Even then there couldn't be much proof. It was quite a clever murder and needed a good deal of patience and determination.'

'Are you seriously asking us to believe,' said Mr Gorringer, glancing towards Moore in the hope of support, 'that the death of Imogen Marvell was in no way connected with these blackmailing villains whom we have now laid by the heels?'

'Only very indirectly. They gave her an emetic in order to force Rolland to pay protection money. It was through the effects of that emetic that Imogen Marvell got herself into a condition to make an injection advisable and give Trudge and Grace the opportunity they wanted. That was the only connection. I can find no evidence at all that Imogen herself was being blackmailed or, as Mrs de Mornay more credibly suggested, was working with the blackmailers. She was a victim of the hatred she inspired in her followers and their greed for her money.'

'Remarkable!' said Mr Gorringer. 'One might say astounding.'

'Not really,' said Carolus. 'Is human nature ever really astounding? There are plenty of precedents, I am sure, even for Imogen herself. But I hope I may never see blue ribbon again.'